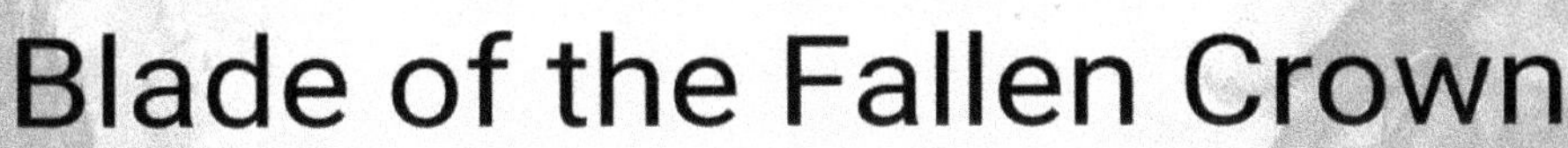

Blade of the Fallen Crown

Volume 1: The Exile and the Blade

(Prologue - The Betrayal)

The sun dipped low over the horizon, setting the skies of Elaria ablaze with hues of gold and crimson. From the clouds above, the kingdom stretched like a dream painted in light and magic, ivory towers laced with glowing runes, wyverns soaring lazily in the warm twilight. It was a realm of wonder and peace.
And yet, beneath the splendor, shadows stirred.

Inside the royal nursery, serenity reigned. Queen Seraphina sat by the tall arched windows, the light of sunset gently tracing the edges of her silken gown. She cradled her newborn son in her arms, his silver eyes wide with innocent curiosity.

"He'll be kind," she whispered, brushing a golden curl from the baby's brow. "Strong... a beacon for our people."

Behind her, King Aureon watched with quiet pride that reached deeper than words. His long crimson cloak shimmered with enchantment, and the weight of both crown and fatherhood sat heavy on his shoulders.

"He carries the blood of dragons and kings," Aureon murmured. "He must be."

The baby gurgled happily, grasping at the king's outstretched finger with surprising strength. A smile broke across the monarch's face.

Yet far below the gentle lullabies and soft laughter, someone else watched.

Beyond the palace walls, shrouded in shadows, stood a lone figure. He wore noble robes of deep sapphire, his silver hair neatly tied back, but his presence was anything but serene. His eyes, once filled with loyalty, were now distant and cold.

Lord Malrik.

Once the king's most trusted advisor. Once commander of the Arcane Guard. Once a friend.
Now, something else entirely.

He said nothing as he turned and walked into the dusk.

The memory came unbidden, years buried, yet still alive in Malrik's mind like a scar that refused to fade.

They had once sparred together beneath the open skies of Elaria's western courtyard. Two boys drenched in sweat and laughter, swinging wooden blades with youthful pride. The clang of their practice swords rang out like music, echoed by the cheers of watching soldiers.

Aureon was always the bolder one, wild and radiant. He fought with the spirit of a prince and the heart of a lion. Malrik, ever calculating, answered with precision and strategy. Where Aureon danced with fire, Malrik wielded ice.

Watching from the stone steps was another boy, silent, broad-shouldered, and already imposing even in his youth. Thorne. Arms crossed, face unreadable. A quiet storm.

Those days were simple. Honest. Before the rot.
Before Aureon chose peace over strength.

Malrik blinked the memory away as his boots echoed down the stone corridor of the royal palace. The torches on the walls flickered, casting his shadow in jagged patterns along the marble. There was no warmth in this hall now, only silence and the faint hum of magic that pulsed with unease.

The guards did not speak to him. They knew better. His presence had grown colder with each passing year, his robes darker, his words sharper. He had not been the same man since the day he realized the truth.

Elaria was dying.
Not by sword or siege, but by softness. By compromise. Magic, once revered, was now shackled by law. Great beasts driven away, relics sealed, power diluted in the name of diplomacy.

Aureon had caged the soul of the kingdom. And Malrik would set it free.

He came to a stop before a door carved with ancient glyphs. A whisper of power slithered beneath the wood like smoke. He pressed his palm to the runes. The seal gave way with a hiss, and the door creaked open into the darkness.

Inside, shadowed figures emerged from the gloom, faces hidden beneath hoods stitched with arcane thread. The Circle. Loyal only to him now.

One of them stepped forward, bearing an obsidian blade inscribed with corrupted runes that pulsed like a dying heart.

"Swear it, Malrik," the figure rasped. "No turning back."

Malrik took the blade without hesitation. It was heavy with fate. His voice was quiet, "finally I will rebuild this kingdom in my image."

The throne room of Elaria was carved from dragon bone and rune-etched obsidian, a chamber where magic and might coexisted in perfect harmony. It was a place built for kings, not just to rule, but to remember the weight of what came before.

King Aureon stood at the war table, eyes narrowed over a map of the borderlands. His fingertips traced the edges of regions marked with flickering enchantments, areas that should have been dormant.

But the land itself was stirring. Rumors spoke of twisted creatures, storms that defied the wind, whispers in the dark that chilled even seasoned scouts.

“This magic,” Aureon murmured, “it isn’t natural.”

Across from him stood General Thorne, a towering presence clad in battle-worn armor. His cloak was torn, his gauntlets scratched, and a great sword rested against his back like a pillar of iron judgment. He leaned over the map with furrowed brows.

“Then we strike,” Thorne said, his voice gravel and thunder. “Wipe it out before it spreads.”

Aureon didn’t respond immediately. He watched his friend, the man who had saved his life more times than he could count, who had stood with him on blood-soaked fields, who had held the line when others fled. And yet, his thoughts were elsewhere.

“There’s unrest within the High Circle,” the king said at last. “Too many voices clamoring for change. Too many shadows behind smiles.”

Thorne’s gaze sharpened. “You’re speaking of Malrik.”

The name hovered in the air like a blade unsheathed.

Aureon exhaled slowly. “He believes peace has made us weak. That our restraint is cowardice.”

“He’s wrong.” Thorne’s fist clenched on the edge of the table. “He forgets what war cost us, what we bled to protect.”

Aureon looked away, the lines on his face deeper now, his golden eyes dimmed by a storm he could not yet name.

“I fear,” he said softly, “the true threat is closer than we know.”

Night fell like a veil over Elaria, draping the kingdom in an uneasy hush.

The palace, once alive with song and arcane light, now whispered only silence. Guards stood at half-attention, lulled by the late hour.

The enchanted sconces that lined the halls dimmed slightly, their usual brilliance flickering with shadows that clung too tightly to the walls.

Footsteps echoed in the gloom.

Lord Malrik moved like a wraith through the corridors, clad in ceremonial armor as dark as onyx, etched with blood-red glyphs that shimmered with forbidden magic. His cloak trailed behind him like flowing smoke. He passed by two sentries at the throne room gate.

He raised his hand.

With a soft murmur, runes flared in the air around his fingers. The guards collapsed without a sound.

WHUUUMM.

One by one, the defenses of the royal palace crumbled, not by siege but by silence. In her private chambers, Queen Seraphina stirred.
A shiver rippled through her skin as she held baby Kael tightly against her chest. The air was wrong. The stillness wasn't peace; it was a warning.

"Aureon…" she whispered, rising from her chair and moving toward the window. "Something's wrong."

Outside, the stars blinked behind clouds like eyes hiding behind a veil. The wind carried no music. Only dread.

Then, without warning, the great doors of the throne room exploded inward in a cascade of flame and shadow.
KRAKOOM!

Aureon rose from his throne in a single motion, blade drawn. His royal sword, Solbrand, shimmered with Sunfire. He did not hesitate.

"Malrik!" he roared, his voice ringing across marble. "You dare bring war beneath this roof?"

Malrik stepped into the throne room like a prophet walking into a temple.
Behind him came his corrupted Arcane Guard, once noble mages now twisted by the shadow arts. Beside them slithered creatures born of nightmare, shadow beasts whose forms were half flesh, half smoke.

"You let weakness rule this land," Malrik said coldly. "I will save it… without you."

He drew his blade, jagged, blackened, and alive with cursed energy. It moaned like a wounded spirit, and the throne room darkened.

Steel met steel. The king lunged. **Clang!**
The two blades clashed, sending sparks of light and shadow into the air. The battle of ideals, of brothers turned rivals, began with fury.

From the side corridors, Thorne entered the fray without pause. His great sword howled as it cut through two corrupted guards in a single sweep.

"Seraphina!" he bellowed. "Take the prince and go!"

"No!" she cried, eyes blazing. "Thorne, take him! Run! RUN!"

Another explosion rocked the palace. The foundation quaked. Kael wailed in his mother's arms, his cries sharp and terrified.

Thorne hesitated, but only for a second. Then he reached for the prince.
He lifted the child into his arms, the baby's cries echoing like war drums across the collapsing palace.

He gave Queen Seraphina one last look, a silent farewell between warriors. She nodded, radiant even in the face of doom. Her hands were already glowing with divine magic, ready to defend her home one final time.
Thorne turned and ran.

The hidden passage opened with a pulse of old magic. Runes ignited along the stone corridor, lighting his way through the bowels of the palace and toward the forest beyond. Behind him, the sounds of chaos thundered, clashing steel, shouts of fury, and the roar of spells tearing the world apart.

Meanwhile, in the throne room, King Aureon and Malrik continued their deadly dance.
The king was fast, his blade guided by decades of training and arcane might. But Malrik had become something else entirely. Twisted by dark power, he fought like a man possessed, a man with nothing to lose.

Aureon feinted low, but Malrik's spell caught him off guard. Black flame erupted beneath the king's feet.
He stumbled just enough. Malrik's blade found its mark.
The cursed steel punched through Aureon's side, crackling with energy that seared flesh and soul alike.

The king gasped, blood on his lips.
But he still stood. Still held his blade.

"May our son return," he rasped, "and end you."

Malrik said nothing. His expression did not even flicker.
Aureon collapsed.

Elsewhere in the burning palace, Queen Seraphina faced the onslaught alone.
Her hands glowed with radiant fire as she tore through shadow beasts one after another. Her eyes blazed with sorrow and fury, her magic fueled by love, by defiance, by the knowledge that her child still breathed.

One last blast of light incinerated a corrupted mage, turning the corridor white-hot. Then a bolt of dark energy struck her from behind.
She staggered, eyes wide, and fell.

Far below, deep in the palace's hidden ways, Thorne stumbled into the forest beyond the city walls. His lungs burned, his armor was scorched, and Kael still cried in his arms.
The night air was cool, the stars obscured by the smoke rising from the distant palace.

He paused only once. He looked back for a heartbeat. There, in the distance, the tower of Elaria burned. A single tear slipped down Thorne's weathered face.
He turned away and disappeared into the woods.

The fires burned for three days.
From the highest spire of the royal palace, black smoke spiraled into the heavens like a wound in the sky. The city of Elaria stood in stunned silence. Whispers filled the streets, rumors of monsters, betrayal, and a magical accident none could explain.

But when Lord Malrik stood before the people, draped in radiant white armor and flanked by solemn-faced mages, there was only grief in his eyes.
Or so they believed.

"King Aureon died defending the palace from a magical rupture," he said, his voice steady, heavy with practiced sorrow. "Queen Seraphina perished alongside him. A tragedy beyond words."

His hand reached out, not to plead but to claim.
"In the absence of an heir, I accept the burden of the crown. For Elaria. For peace."

The crowd watched, uncertain. Some wept. Others bowed. But one man in the back did neither.
Cloaked in brown, face hidden beneath his hood, General Thorne stood among the people, unmoving. A bundle in his arms shifted softly, an infant, now quiet, eyes wide and blue as flame.

Malrik's eyes swept the crowd briefly, then moved on.
Thorne turned without a word and vanished into the edge of the woods. He would not forget.

They lived in a hollowed-out tree, tucked deep in the wildwood. Time passed slowly there. The world would forget it existed. He would raise Kael not as a prince, but as a survivor.

"You'll learn every blade," Thorne whispered once, laying his great sword beside Kael's crib. "Every spell. You'll be stronger than all of us."

And far away, in the halls of obsidian and fire, King Malrik sat upon the throne with a kingdom bound to his will.
But truth, no matter how deeply buried, stirs eventually.
And beneath the ashes of betrayal waited the heir to a broken crown. The spark of a rebellion.

This is how legends are born.

Chapter 1 - Forged in the Wild

The Whispering Wilds were not kind to men, and even less kind to babes. Thorne learned that on the very first night.
The child would not stop crying. His cries pierced the hollowed oak they had taken shelter in, sharp as any blade, cutting through the hardened general's nerves. Thorne, who had once commanded legions, who had faced trolls, demons, and Malrik's horrors, now found himself utterly undone by a squalling newborn.

"By God, boy," Thorne muttered, pacing the dirt floor with the tiny bundle in his arms. "You're smaller than my gauntlet and louder than a war horn."

Kael's wails did not soften.

Thorne tried feeding him again from the goat's milk he had bartered for before fleeing into the wilds, but half of it spilled down the boy's chin. He tried rocking him, bouncing him, even singing a deep, gravelly mutter of an old soldier's march. Nothing worked.

At last, Thorne sank down by the cold hearth, cradling Kael close against his chest. His scarred hands looked too large, too rough for something so fragile.
"I don't know what I'm doing," he confessed aloud, voice barely above a whisper. "I was made to wield steel, not raise kings. Your father... he would have known what to say. Your mother." His throat closed, and for a moment, the war hound's one good eye burned. "But they're gone. And it's just me. Just us."

Kael's crying softened into hiccups, then into restless whimpers. Eventually, the boy slept, and Thorne sat unmoving for hours, afraid that if he shifted even once, the fragile miracle in his arms might shatter.

It was the first time in decades the general had prayed. Not to God, but to the spirits of the dead. Help me keep him alive.

The days that followed tested Thorne more than any battle ever had.

Kael seemed determined to die, or so it felt. He refused the milk half the time, wailed at the smallest noises, and had a habit of wriggling free of his wrappings at the worst possible moment. Once, when Thorne turned for a heartbeat to stoke the fire, the boy rolled dangerously close to the edge of the bedding. The general's heart nearly burst from his chest as he snatched the child back into his arms.

"You'll be the death of me," he growled. But the boy only blinked up at him with wide, blue eyes, his mother's eyes, and Thorne's anger dissolved.

He learned, awkwardly, how to soothe him. A slow rhythm of steps around the hollow's interior seemed to calm him best. Humming the old march helped, though Thorne would never admit it. He fashioned a crude cradle from woven branches, lined with moss, though Kael always seemed to prefer his chest.

Food was another battle. Thorne, who had lived half his life on soldier's rations, found himself hunting daily, not just for himself but for the milk-giving goat he had bartered from a terrified villager during their flight. He built snares, foraged berries, even bartered with dangerous forest folk for herbs when Kael grew feverish one night.

That fever nearly broke him.

The boy had burned hot against his arm, skin slick with sweat, tiny body writhing with cries that sounded weaker by the hour.

Thorne, helpless, plunged him into a stream's cold shallows while whispering rough prayers. He carried him through the night, pressing herbs between Kael's lips, begging the child not to leave him.

When dawn came, the fever broke. Kael slept, breathing soft and steady, his chest rising and falling with stubborn strength.

Thorne wept then, though no one was there to see.
"You're your father's son," he said thickly, pressing a hand to his face. "Too stubborn to die."

From that day forward, Kael's cries no longer sounded like torment to Thorne. They sounded like defiance, like life itself refusing to be snuffed out.

Years blurred in the Wilds.
Kael grew, first crawling across mossy floors, then staggering on uncertain legs. His first word was not "father," nor "mama," but a garbled, determined attempt at "sword."

Thorne laughed until his ribs ached, though secretly it made his heart heavy too.

By the age of five, Kael followed Thorne on short hunts, carrying sticks twice his size, pretending they were spears. By six, he could climb the lower branches of the ancient trees, dangling like a mischievous sprite while Thorne barked at him to come down. By seven, he had stolen one of Thorne's daggers and nearly cut his own hand open.

And by eight, Thorne decided it was time to begin.

They stood in a small clearing beneath a canopy of whispering leaves, sunlight dappling through in shifting fragments. Kael clutched a wooden sword, crudely carved but balanced enough. His brow furrowed with determination, his stance wide but unsteady.

Thorne loomed before him, scarred arms folded, watching every twitch of the boy's muscles.
"First lesson," he said. "Your feet. The ground will kill you faster than any blade if you trip. Balance."

Kael shuffled his stance, mimicking what he had seen Thorne do countless times. "Better," Thorne grunted. "Now strike."

Kael lunged. It was wild, clumsy, and left his chest open. Thorne tapped him lightly in the ribs with the flat of his great sword.
"Dead," the general said.

Kael scowled. "That's not fair! You're faster!"
"I'm alive," Thorne countered. "That's what matters."

So began the training. Day after day, Kael swung his wooden sword until his arms ached. Thorne taught him the rhythm of combat: feint, strike, retreat, breathe. He drilled footwork until Kael stumbled into bed at night too sore to move. And still, the boy rose each morning with fire in his eyes.

It was during one of those evenings, after another bruising lesson, that Kael asked. They sat by the fire in the hollow oak, stew bubbling in the pot, shadows dancing against the bark. Kael stared into the flames, sword resting across his knees.
"Tell me about them," he said suddenly. Thorne looked up from the stew. "Them?"
"My parents."

Silence stretched. The only sound was the crackle of firewood and the whisper of wind through the cracks in the tree.

Thorne set down the ladle, his face unreadable in the firelight.
"You've heard the stories."
"I want to hear them again."

Thorne studied him for a long time. Then he nodded, as he always did.
"Your father," he said slowly, "was the strongest man I ever knew. Not just in battle, but in spirit. He led from the front, bled with his soldiers, never gave in to fear or pride. When the time came, he stood against Malrik without hesitation. Fought like a lion until the end."

Kael's jaw tensed. "And my mother?"
Thorne's voice softened, almost reverent. "She was the soul of the kingdom.

A seer, a healer, a queen who saw everyone, even a battle-hardened war hound like me, as worth saving. She gave her life to protect you."

Kael stared into the fire, sword trembling in his hands. "They died because of me."

Thorne's eye narrowed. "No. They died because Malrik is a butcher. You were their hope, boy. Their reason to fight. Don't ever twist that into shame."

The boy swallowed, eyes burning. He said nothing more, but when he finally lay down that night, Thorne heard him whisper to himself, "I'll kill him one day."

Two years passed.

Kael grew taller, faster, sharper. The sword in his hand became an extension of his arm, his feet steadier, his strikes truer. At ten years old, he was no soldier, but he was no child either.

It was raining the night he finally struck Thorne. The clearing was slick with mud, droplets cascading from the leaves above. Kael's hair clung wet to his forehead, his wooden sword gripped tight. He moved with the rhythm Thorne had drilled into him: feint high, strike low, pivot left, stab. His eyes never left his opponent.

Thorne blocked each blow with practiced ease, though now he had to work for it. Then Kael slipped through. A sudden shift, a feint that flowed cleaner than before. His sword tapped against Thorne's shoulder.

The general grunted, taking half a step back. Kael blinked, stunned. “I... I hit you.”
Thorne raised a brow. “Again.”

Kael attacked without thinking, pressing harder, faster, each strike laced with fury and determination. Thorne blocked, parried, countered, until at last he swept Kael’s legs from beneath him. The boy hit the mud with a grunt.

But instead of lying there defeated, he grinned up at the storm. “I almost got you.”

Thorne offered a hand, hauling him up. “You’re getting faster,” he admitted. Then, gruffly, “Don’t get cocky.”

Kael’s eyes gleamed. “Wasn’t that almost praise?”
“Don’t push your luck,” Thorne replied.

That night, as rain pattered against the hollow oak’s roof, Kael sat awake, staring into the fire. The sword rested beside him, its wooden blade worn smooth by his grip. He thought of his father and mother, their faces blurred but their sacrifice sharp as steel. He thought of Malrik, whose shadow hung over every story, every scar in Thorne’s voice.

Kael’s small fingers curled into fists. “I’ll take it back,” he whispered to the flames. “The kingdom. The crown. Everything he stole. I’ll make him pay.”

Thorne sat across from him, silent, watching. He did not speak or correct him this time. Because in Kael's eyes, for the first time, he saw not a boy with a wooden sword, but the beginning of a king.

Chapter 2 - The Arrow in the Wild

The day Kael met Lyra, he almost lost an eye.

He had wandered farther than he meant to, following the faint tracks of a stag through the Whispering Wilds. At eighteen, he had long since learned how to move like the forest itself: quiet, measured, each step tested before he placed weight upon it. The moss softened his tread, the damp air carried his breath in white veils, and the steady rhythm of his pulse echoed the old lessons Thorne had carved into him with bark-hard discipline. Hunt with your eyes, not your ears. Trust your instincts. Never lose your footing.

Kael carried himself with the quiet confidence of a hunter, but beneath that calm lay a storm, the endless drive that had been hammered into his bones since childhood. The Wilds had raised him as much as Thorne had, and though he was not yet a king, he already moved like one destined for battle.

He crouched at the base of a gnarled oak, tracing the faint indent of a hoofprint in the damp earth. His hand brushed the hilt of his sword, not because he needed it, but because he always did. He had grown used to the weight of steel at his side; it was as much a part of him now as breath.

That was when the arrow came.

It hissed through the air, fast as lightning and silent as a serpent. Kael's instincts saved him. His head jerked aside a fraction before impact, and the shaft buried itself in the bark beside him, quivering from the force of its flight. Had he moved a heartbeat slower, it would have taken his eye clean out.

Kael dropped low, sword clearing its sheath with a metallic whisper. His breath came sharp, eyes narrowing as he scanned the trees. Nothing moved. No sound but the faint rustle of leaves overhead.

The forest was always full of whispers, but the silence now was different, an expectant hush that came before blood was spilled.

“Show yourself!” Kael barked, his voice sharper than he intended. His heart hammered in his chest, but his stance held steady. He raised the blade, angled low, ready to strike. “I’m not your prey.”

For a moment, nothing. Then, from above, a voice like soft steel. “Then don't move like one.”

The figure dropped from the branches in a blur of green and shadow. She landed with a grace that made no sound, the bow already lowered but strung, her hand resting on the fletching of another arrow. Her cloak shifted with her movement, woven in mottled green and black that blended with the Wilds themselves. Long silver-blonde hair fell from a loose braid over one shoulder, catching the faint strands of light that broke through the canopy.

An elf.

Kael tensed. Thorne’s warnings echoed in his skull: Never trust easily. Some would sell your blood for coin, others for revenge. The elves remember the wars. Not all forgive.

Her eyes caught him, sharp and calculating, the pale hue of stormlight over water. A thin scar ran through her left eyebrow, giving her face a dangerous tilt, a reminder of a battle survived. She looked young, perhaps twenty, but there was no innocence in her stance. She moved like someone who had lived twice as long.

“You’re trespassing,” she said, her voice quiet but unyielding. “This part of the Wilds belongs to no one.”

Kael's sword lowered slightly, though his body stayed coiled like a spring. "I wasn't aware the trees were yours."

"I didn't say they were mine." Her lips curved faintly, though not in kindness. "I said they weren't yours."

Her bow caught his attention then. It was unlike any weapon Kael had seen: pale wood, polished smooth but etched with faint runes that shimmered in the light, carved into the limbs of the bow itself. The string gleamed like woven silver sinew, taut as if it sang even without an arrow drawn. This was no simple hunter's tool; it was art, heritage, and death given form.

Kael forced himself to hold her gaze instead of staring at it. "I'm not here to steal," he said carefully. "Just scouting for deer."

She tilted her head, studying him. "You don't smell like a poacher or a bandit." Her eyes flicked over him, as though measuring every scar and every line of tension in his body. "You smell like smoke and steel... and wet moss."

Kael blinked, caught off guard. "I live nearby."

Her stare sharpened. "With who?"

"My mentor."

"Name?"

Kael hesitated. Names carried weight. But he was not ashamed of Thorne. "Thorne."

The name struck something in her; her brow lifted a fraction. "The Butcher of Irondeep?"

The old wound of that name burned hot in Kael's chest. His grip tightened on the hilt of his sword. "That title doesn't mean what people think it does."

"Oh, I'm sure it doesn't." The faint curve of her mouth sharpened into a smirk. "They rarely do."

Then she turned, as fluid as the wind, and began to walk away. She slipped between the trees like a shadow returning to its source, as though the forest itself bent to let her pass.

"Wait," Kael said, moving before he could stop himself, weaving between brambles to keep her in sight. "Who are you?"

She glanced back over her shoulder, her braid catching on the breeze. Her eyes locked with his, unreadable.

"Lyra."

"That's it?"

"That's all you've earned." And she was gone.

Kael stood in the hush of the Wilds, his sword still loose in his hand, his breath shallow with the adrenaline that refused to leave his blood. He replayed every detail of her in his mind: the scar, the way she had drawn on him without hesitation, the sharpness of her gaze that had seen too much.

He sheathed his blade slowly, forcing his heart to settle.

That night, Kael sat by the fire with Thorne, the flames painting shadows across the hollow of their shelter. Thorne grunted beside him as he skinned a rabbit, the knife flashing in his calloused hands.

"You hesitated," the old general said without looking up.

Kael frowned. "She didn't mean to kill me."

"She meant to scare you," Thorne muttered. "Which means she thought she could."

Kael's jaw tightened. He stared into the fire. "She was fast. Fluid. Every step... like it was practiced a hundred times."

Thorne's knife slowed. "She has practiced a hundred times." His tone was low, edged with something between respect and disdain. "Lyra of the Whispering Ash. Half the bounty guilds in the south have her name on a scroll. Mercenary. Tracker. Marksman. Most only know her by the stories."

Kael blinked, startled. "She didn't seem like a killer."

Thorne snorted. "That's the point."

But Kael couldn't shake the thought. He had seen killers before, seen the coldness in their eyes, the hollowness that came when blood was just another coin's weight.

Lyra's eyes weren't hollow. They were sharp, yes, and wary. But beneath that suspicion was something else, an old ache, maybe even loneliness.

"She could've left me alone," Kael said quietly. "Or robbed me. But she warned me. Gave me her name. That means something."

Thorne was silent for a long while, tossing the rabbit's skin aside. Finally, he muttered, "You're thinking about asking her to join us."

Kael shook his head. "Not yet. But I want to know more."

Elsewhere, in the deeper reaches of the Wilds, Lyra sat alone upon a mossy stone. She had built a fire, no more than a flicker, just enough to dry her damp leathers and chase away the creeping cold. Her bow lay across her lap, pale and flawless, though faint scratches lined the runes, marks of battles survived.

She traced one with her thumb absentmindedly. The string gleamed faintly in the firelight, taut as ever. It was her most prized possession, passed from her mother before death had stolen her too young. Every mark upon it was a memory, every scar, every escape.

She should have forgotten the boy already. She had met countless men in these woods, and most were worth less than the fletching of an arrow. But something about him lingered.

His stance. The way he moved, all discipline and tension. The way his eyes burned, storm-dark and defiant.

He hadn't moved like a poacher or a thief. He hadn't carried himself like a prince either, despite the nobility etched in the lines of his jaw. No, he moved like someone preparing for war.

Lyra leaned back, exhaling. "Trouble," she murmured. And trouble always had a way of finding her.

Interlude-The Serpent on the Throne

The throne room of Castle Noctis was nothing like the hall that had once ruled the heart of the realm.
It did not carry the scent of roses or incense; it reeked of blood, smoke, and cold iron.

Once, Castle Aurelia had stood proud at the center of Elaria City, a beacon of light, its marble halls alive with laughter, music, and the warmth of its people. The stained-glass windows had glimmered with morning light, casting colors over the polished floors as children ran through the courtyards. Merchants, knights, and farmers all looked upon that castle and saw hope.

But now, Castle Aurelia is a corpse. A hollow shell.
Its halls were cold, its towers cracked, its light extinguished. The people who still lived in the city could see its shadow each day, and with it, they remembered what had been taken from them.

Far from that once-glorious heart, buried deep within the jagged Hollow Mountains, rose Malrik's new fortress, Castle Noctis. It was carved into the black stone itself, a fortress of spikes and shadow, built not to inspire but to intimidate. A throne of terror had replaced a throne of light.

Lord Malrik sat upon the jagged obsidian throne he had stolen, fingers laced before him, his pale eyes half-lidded in mock boredom as a court of cowards and killers groveled at his feet.

The crown on his brow was not the diadem of Elaria's kings. That one had been melted down long ago, its gold reforged into the hilts of assassins' daggers. The new crown was sharp, cruel, and black as midnight, fitting for the serpent who wore it.

“Another rebellion in the east,” muttered a thin man in ink-stained robes, clutching a scroll like a shield. “A farming village claiming the boy still lives.”

Malrik’s gaze flicked toward him, those pale, glassy eyes stripped of the last remnants of humanity by the pact he had made.

“Kill the elders. Hang them in the square,” Malrik said softly. “Salt the fields. Let the next village grow their wheat over bones if they wish to speak of ghosts.”

“My lord, the grain,” the advisor began weakly.

Malrik waved a hand. “Will be replaced by the south. I do not rule with bread. I rule by fear.”

Behind the throne stood figures wrapped in black and crimson, the Order of the Crimson Veil. Their bone masks hid their faces, but their presence poisoned the air. Across Elaria, their name alone was enough to silence children’s cries and stop a mother’s prayer.

Malrik rose slowly and approached a tall archway that overlooked the dark world below. From Castle Noctis, the peaks stretched endlessly, speared with watchtowers pulsing with unnatural light. The land beyond lay like a kingdom in shadow.
And far in the distance, barely visible on the horizon, the broken outline of Castle Aurelia still stood, a scar against the sky.

A smile ghosted across Malrik’s lips. Elaria bent to his will. But the shadow in his mind never left him.

He had hunted for years, sent assassins, burned villages, scoured forests and mountains. But no matter how far he reached, the boy remained a phantom.

Kael.

He never spoke the name aloud.

The few seers he had spared had whispered the same prophecy with their dying breaths: “The heir of fire shall return.”

His lip curled in disdain. He despised prophecies. They gave fools courage. They gave peasants hope.

But when the boy finally revealed himself, and Malrik knew he would, he would fall like the rest.
Just another ember crushed beneath a serpent’s heel.

Chapter 3 - Fangs in the Fog

The smoke came with the dawn.

Kael smelled it before he saw it, woodsmoke laced with blood. It drifted through the trees in thick coils, carried on a breeze too warm for morning. By the time he crested the ridge, bow in hand, the sky was already turning red.

Below, the village burned.

It was a small settlement on the outskirts of the Whispering Wilds, mostly thatched-roof homes and modest crop fields. Farmers. Simple folk. Not warriors.
Which made the shrieking sound echoing through the valley all the more terrifying.

Kael crouched low behind the brush and nocked an arrow. He wasn't a master with the bow, since Thorne had made sure he focused on sword and dagger first, but it was better than nothing.

Then the ground rumbled.

They came out of the fog like phantoms: great, hulking beasts with jagged teeth and bone-covered hides. Eyes like glowing embers. Maws wide with unnatural hunger.

Direfangs.

Kael's blood ran cold. These weren't simple forest predators. These were corrupted beasts, twisted by dark magic, their natural instincts overridden by bloodlust.
They weren't hunting. They were sent.

Kael didn't think. He drew, aimed, and loosed.

His arrow struck one Direfang in the neck, not a kill, but enough to stagger it. The creature turned toward him, snarling.

"Well," a familiar voice said behind him, "you really know how to start the day off loud."

Kael spun, startled. Lyra stood with her bow already drawn, eyes narrowed, hair pulled back in a tight braid. Her expression was calm but alert.

"You followed me," he said.

"No," she replied. "I followed them. You just happen to be in the way."

Another Direfang burst from the trees, barreling straight toward them. Kael dropped his bow and drew his sword and dagger in one fluid motion.

"Left!" he shouted. "I'll take center!"

Lyra didn't argue. She moved like wind and shadow, disappearing into the underbrush as Kael met the beast head-on. Steel met fang.

Kael ducked a swipe, slashed across its ribs, and rolled clear of its crushing bite. He stabbed upward with his dagger, driving it into the beast's eye just as Lyra's arrow pierced its throat from behind. It collapsed in a heap.

Breathing hard, Kael looked up to see Lyra already lining up her next shot.

"I'm beginning to think you enjoy this," he said.

"I enjoy not dying," she shot back.

The village below was chaos, screaming families, panicked animals, homes aflame.
Two more Direfangs tore through the main road. A group of villagers tried to fight back with pitchforks, but they wouldn't last long.

Kael and Lyra didn't speak. They ran.

Kael hit the first Direfang like a hammer, diving from a rooftop with both blades drawn. He struck true, his sword slicing deep into the beast's spine. It howled and flung him aside with a brutal backhanded swipe.

He slammed into a pile of firewood. Pain exploded through his ribs.

Lyra took the opening, three quick arrows, each finding a soft point in the creature's throat and chest. It dropped like a felled tree.

Kael staggered to his feet.

"Third one, clockwise," Lyra warned, already moving again.

Kael followed her gaze. The last Direfang was charging toward a group of children huddled behind an overturned cart.

No time to flank. No time to think. Kael sprinted.

The creature saw him, turned, and roared.

Kael jumped, planted his foot on the cart, and launched himself into the air. His blade sang as he came down on the beast's skull with all his strength, driving the edge deep into bone and brain. The Direfang fell still.

Silence returned, broken only by the crackle of flames and the sobbing of survivors. Kael stood over the body, chest heaving, blood dripping from his sword.

Lyra walked up beside him. Her expression was unreadable.

"Well," she said after a moment, "you're either insane or incredibly lucky."

Kael wiped his blade on the beast's fur. "Bit of both."

One of the villagers approached, a grizzled man with soot on his face and tears in his eyes.

"Thank the stars," he whispered. "You saved us."

Kael sheathed his sword. "Who sent the beasts?"

The man shook his head. "Don't know. They came before dawn. But... one of them wore armor."

Kael's eyes darkened. "They were controlled."

Lyra looked toward the horizon. "That's not random. That's a test run."

Kael nodded. "And someone's watching."

They made camp on the edge of the village ruins. Kael sat cleaning his blades while Lyra tended to a small fire. For the first time, neither spoke in sarcasm nor challenge.
They had fought together. Bled together.
There was a strange kind of understanding in that.

"I saw the way you moved today," Kael said finally. "You've fought beasts like that before."

“I’ve fought worse,” Lyra replied, staring into the flames. “And I’ve seen where they come from.”

Kael glanced over.

She didn’t offer more. And he didn’t press.

Instead, he said, “We could use someone like you.”

Lyra chuckled softly. “We, huh? Thought you and tree giant were lone wolves.”

Kael smiled faintly. “Even lone wolves get tired of howling alone.”

He paused then, his gaze distant for a moment, as if weighing whether to speak the next words at all.

“The truth is, I’m not just another wanderer. The kingdom thinks its prince died that night, the night the royal line burned. But I lived, and I’m going to take Elaria back. I just, can’t do it alone.”

She looked at him then, really looked. And for a moment, something flickered in her eyes. Not pity. Not affection. Recognition.

“Alright, prince,” she said, laying back with her hands behind her head. “I’ll stick around. For now. Try not to get yourself killed.”

Kael watched the stars overhead, his muscles sore but his spirit steady.
One ally gained. One step closer.

Chapter 4 - Sparks of Leadership

The trail to their hidden camp was marked by nothing but instinct.
Kael led the way, ducking under low-hanging branches and stepping across a narrow stream that trickled over mossy stones. He did not look back often, but he knew Lyra followed. Quiet as ever, light on her feet, yet with a presence that filled the forest behind him like a second heartbeat.

"She won't like him," Kael muttered to himself.

"Excuse me?" Lyra said, amused.

"Thorne," he replied. "He's not exactly a people person."

Lyra smirked. "Neither am I."

Kael could not argue with that.

They reached the clearing near dusk. The massive hollowed-out tree stood tall in the center, its bark darkened with age, vines curling up its sides like lazy serpents. Smoke rose gently from the small cookfire, and the scent of roasted meat filled the air.

Thorne sat near the flames, sharpening his sword with a whetstone. He did not look up when they entered. He did not have to.

"I heard you before I heard the girl," he grunted. "You're getting sloppy."

Kael grinned. "Maybe I'm getting comfortable."

"You should never be comfortable in the Wilds," Thorne replied, eyes still on his blade.

Lyra stepped forward, arms crossed. "You must be the warm and welcoming mentor I've heard so much about."

Thorne finally looked up. His single eye studied her in silence. "Elf," he said flatly.

"Human," she shot back.

Kael sighed. "And here I thought this would go well."

They ate in silence for a while, seated around the fire as night fell over the forest. Lyra leaned back against a log, one eye half-closed, while Thorne chewed methodically. Kael poked the fire with a stick, waiting.

Finally, Thorne spoke.
"You brought her here. That means you trust her."

Kael nodded.
"She saved villagers. She fights with purpose. And she could have left me to die. Twice."

Lyra looked at him. "I didn't know it was twice."

"You shot at me the first time we met."

"Oh. Right."

Thorne exhaled through his nose, something between a grunt and a laugh. "I've seen elves who kill for coin. She's not one of them."

"I kill for survival," Lyra corrected. "But lately... I've started thinking about something else."

Thorne raised a brow.

She looked directly at Kael.
"About what it would take to change this kingdom."

A long silence followed. Only the fire spoke, crackling between them like it had secrets to tell.

Later that night, Kael stood just beyond the firelight, watching the moon filter through the canopy. The stars above looked like scattered embers, cold and eternal.

He did not notice Thorne approach until the man spoke.
"You brought her here for a reason."

"I didn't plan it," Kael replied.

Thorne nodded slowly. "That's not what I mean."

Kael turned to him. "Then what?"

"You brought her because you need her. Not just for battle. For people."

Kael looked down. "I'm not trying to be their leader, Thorne."

"You don't get to choose," Thorne said quietly. "People follow strength. But they stay for something else."

Kael was silent.

"You've got fire in you, Kael. That will scare some. But if you want to reclaim Elaria, you need more than heat. You need to be the kind of man others believe in. Not just one who swings the sword."

Kael frowned. "I'm not sure I know how to do that."

“Then start by listening,” Thorne said. “And don’t waste the ones who believe in you.”

Later that night, Kael found Lyra sitting on a fallen tree, her bow resting across her lap.

“You didn’t have to stay,” he said.

“I know,” she replied. “But I did.”

They were quiet for a moment.

“You’ve seen the kingdom,” Kael said. “The rot. The fear. The silence.”

Lyra nodded.

“I want to change it,” Kael continued. “Not just reclaim the throne. Not just kill Malrik. I want to rebuild something better.”

Lyra looked at him, searching his face. “And if no one follows you?”

Kael met her gaze. “I’ll still try.”

She smiled, just a little.
“Then I’ll follow you for now, prince.”

Kael did not correct her.

That night, as the fire burned low and the stars blinked in quiet approval, Kael realized something.
He wasn’t just surviving anymore. He was beginning to lead.
Not by command. But by conviction.

But peace around the fire never lasted.

As the flames died down, Lyra finally spoke again, her voice cutting the night like a drawn arrow.
“So this is the camp of the Butcher of Irondeep.”

Kael stiffened, turning sharply to her. “Lyra—"

“What?” she said coolly, her eyes never leaving Thorne. “That’s what he’s called, isn’t it? Whole villages spit his name like poison. I’ve heard it since I was a child.”

Thorne did not flinch. He kept his gaze on the fire, one calloused hand tightening around his sword hilt.

Kael’s voice hardened. “That’s enough.”

“No,” Thorne said at last. His tone wasn’t angry, only tired. “She should know. You should know.”

Kael swallowed. “Thorne...”

The older man leaned forward, shadows deepening the scars across his face. His single eye gleamed in the firelight.

“Irondeep wasn’t a slaughter,” he said. “Not the way the songs claim.”

Lyra’s expression faltered, but she didn’t look away.

“Two years before Malrik took the throne,” Thorne continued, “he sent me to Irondeep. Said rebels had taken the mines. Said they planned to march north and burn the villages if we didn’t stop them. I believed him. I led the king’s soldiers into the tunnels. We fought for days in that black stone. When it was done... when the smoke cleared... it wasn’t rebels lying dead.”

His voice cracked, rough with memory. “It was miners. Families. Men who had only taken up arms because Malrik raised their taxes until they starved.”

Kael's chest tightened.

Thorne's jaw worked, like he was chewing glass. "And when I tried to report the truth, Malrik branded me the butcher. Let the people hate me. Their rage made it easier for him to tighten his grip." He spat into the dirt. "A convenient villain to pave his path to the throne."

The night went still. Even the forest seemed to hold its breath.

Lyra's bow hand loosened slowly. She studied him, not with scorn now, but with something else. Something like recognition.

Kael finally spoke, his voice low. "Why didn't you ever tell me?"

Thorne's eye shifted toward him, heavy with regret. "Because you were just a boy. You didn't need to carry that weight. Not then."

Silence stretched, broken only by the crackle of fire.

Lyra finally broke it, her tone softer than before. "So Malrik made you his monster."

Thorne's lips twisted into something like a smile, though it carried no joy. "People will always hate a monster more than a tyrant. That's how Malrik keeps his power, Kael. He makes them fear shadows, so they don't see the man pulling the strings. Don't ever forget that. Kings play games with blood and names. If you mean to stand against him, you'd best be ready for both."

The fire burned low. The forest held its silence.

And in that moment, Kael felt the truth settle into him like a blade drawn across stone.

Malrik hadn't just stolen his crown.
He had stolen truth itself.
And to reclaim the kingdom, Kael would have to take both back.

Interlude - The Weight of Fire

The night was cold.
Not the kind of cold that froze the skin, but the kind that settled in a man's bones. A quiet chill that crept in when the fire burned low and the shadows grew long.

General Thorne sat alone beneath a leaning pine, a mug of bitter bark tea steaming in his hands.
His sword lay beside him, within arm's reach. It always was.

Across the clearing, Kael and Lyra slept beneath layered furs, young and worn from the day's fight, but breathing easily. The boy had grown. Taller, leaner, sharper in mind and movement. He still made mistakes, but now they were fewer—
and more costly.

Thorne took a sip of tea and grimaced.

Kael wasn't a boy anymore. Not in how he fought. Not in how he carried the weight of his bloodline.
And that scared Thorne more than any beast or blade.

Because boys could be protected.
But kings?
Kings had to bleed.

The fire crackled softly as Thorne reached into his pack and pulled out a worn scrap of parchment. A half-burned fragment, salvaged years ago from the ruins of the royal library.

"When fire returns to blood, the crown shall fall and rise anew."
The prophecy of the dragon blood.

Aureon had hated it.
Seraphina had feared it.
But they had never ignored it.

Kael was the last of the bloodline tied to the dragons, descendants of the flame pact forged in the First Era. Long dormant. Thought symbolic. A metaphor passed through ceremony.

But Thorne had seen what slept beneath the boy's skin. Not just anger. Not just pain.

Power.
Unshaped. Unclaimed. And growing.

He remembered the day Kael had set a tree ablaze with a single shout. He had only been twelve. No spell. No incantation. Just a surge of grief during a sparring session, and the sudden roar of white-hot fire lashing from his palms.

Kael didn't remember much afterward. He had collapsed. Slept for three days.
Thorne hadn't slept at all.

The old general stared into the flames now, their orange glow flickering across his face.

"Am I raising a king?" he murmured. "Or a weapon?"

He hated the question. But he asked it anyway. Because no one else would.

He remembered holding Kael as a newborn, swaddled in royal cloth, as the castle burned behind him. Seraphina's final words still echoed in his ears.

"Raise him strong... but raise him kind."

Thorne had done the first.
But the second? That was harder. Harder in a world which kindness from boys and used it to sharpen their enemies' blades.

Something stirred in the shadows behind him. Not danger, just familiarity.

Lyra stepped from the trees, silent as always. She didn't speak. She simply sat beside him and stared into the fire.

"You're worried," she said after a moment.

"I'm always worried," Thorne replied. "But more now."

Lyra glanced at the sleeping Kael. "He listens to you. That's new."

Thorne grunted. "He's stubborn. But not stupid. He's going to need more than cleverness and swordplay soon."

Lyra didn't answer at first, but her expression grew distant.

"I've seen what happens when power gets ahead of purpose," she said. "He has both. That's rare."

Thorne studied her. "And if he loses it?"

Lyra met his gaze. "Then we don't let him."

The fire snapped again, sending a small spray of embers into the sky.

Thorne closed his eye. He was tired. Too old for wars that hadn't yet happened.
But he would carry the weight as long as Kael needed him.
As long as Elaria needed hope.

The prophecy might speak of fire and rebirth.
But Thorne knew the truth.

For something to rise, something else must burn.

Chapter 5 - Shadows Over Whispering Wilds

The night smelled wrong.

Kael had known the scents of villages since childhood: bread baking in stone ovens, woodsmoke rising from quiet hearths, and the earthy musk of tilled fields. But this was different. Acrid smoke clawed at his nose, bitter and choking. Fire, not for warmth, but for destruction.

From the ridge above the valley, he stared down at the small settlement. Flames licked at thatched rooftops. Screams floated up the hill, high and desperate. Shadows moved among the cottages, carrying steel and torches, their laughter jagged as broken glass.

Malrik's soldiers.

Kael's grip tightened on his sword. The moonlight glimmered on the blade's edge, though his palm was slick with sweat. His chest felt like a drum, pounding and rattling against the weight of choice.

He wanted to charge in. To throw himself into the flames and cut down the men who dared terrorize innocents in his kingdom. But instinct warred with impulse, and beside him crouched the two figures who grounded him in the storm.

Thorne spoke first, his gravelly voice a calm blade slicing through the tension.
"Three groups. One ransacking the market square, another dragging folk from their homes, and a third holding the tower. Not raiders. Trained soldiers, though not disciplined." His old soldier's eye gleamed faintly in the firelight, sharp and steady as ever.

Lyra crouched lower, stringing her bow in silence. Her eyes flicked across the chaos below, calculating. “If we hit head-on, we’ll be crushed. But strike fast, split them before they rally, and we might stand a chance. The villagers will fight if they see hope.”

Her voice held no tremor, though Kael caught the faint crease in her brow. She had seen slaughter before, more than she ever admitted.

Kael swallowed. His tongue felt heavy, the weight of command pressing harder than the sword at his hip. He had trained all his life for this, but training did not prepare anyone for children's cries piercing the night, or seeing your people dragged into the dirt.

His throat burned. He forced himself to speak.
“Thorne, the market. Keep them pinned. Don't let them scatter. Lyra, with me. We’ll draw the ones at the homes. Once we pull them away, we regroup at the tower and cut off their retreat.”

The silence after his words was sharp as steel.

Then Thorne gave a single nod, pride flickering briefly across his scarred face.
“Sound strategy. Let’s make it bleed.”

Lyra’s eyes lingered on Kael for a breath longer, unreadable. Then she nodded as well, her bowstring thrumming softly as she readied an arrow.

Kael exhaled, tension leaving his chest with the breath. He could not let them see his doubt. If he faltered, they would too.

“Move,” Thorne growled.

They split like shadows into fire.

Kael and Lyra darted between cottages, embers drifting like fireflies around them. A soldier's torch painted the night orange as he dragged a farmer from his doorway.

Kael surged forward, sword flashing in the dark. He struck before the soldier even turned, the blade biting through leather and flesh. The man dropped, the torch tumbling to the dirt.

The farmer froze, staring, then stumbled back as Kael barked, “Run. Get the others clear.”

The farmer hesitated only a heartbeat before vanishing into the smoke.

Two more soldiers turned, steel glinting. One charged Kael, blade raised. The other lunged for Lyra.

Kael’s training took over. The world slowed. His opponent’s sword arced toward him, too high, too eager. Kael dropped low, shoulder slamming into the man's gut. He drove him against the burning wall. The soldier gasped, slackening just enough for Kael to thrust, steel sliding between ribs.

A scream behind him. Lyra spun, her dagger flashing like quicksilver. She caught the second soldier’s wrist mid-swing, twisted, and shoved him off balance. In the same motion, she ducked aside and loosed an arrow at point-blank range into his throat.

Blood sprayed across the dirt. Lyra did not flinch.

Kael stared for a breath too long at her calm, at her precision. Then he yanked his blade free, chest heaving.

“More coming,” she warned.

He nodded and forced his feet to move.

In the market square, chaos reigned. Villagers screamed as soldiers overturned carts, torches blazing. But Thorne was already among them.

Kael glimpsed him briefly through the smoke, the old knight moving with terrifying grace, his great sword carving through the crowd. One man fell, then another, his movements economical and merciless.

And the villagers, emboldened by the sight of someone standing and fighting, began to rise too. Men with pitchforks, women with cleavers, even children hurling stones. Fear turned to fury, and fury to action.

Kael's chest tightened. This was what leadership could spark. Not just survival, but defiance.

Then the tower. Kael, Lyra, and Thorne converged at its base, where the last group of soldiers had gathered. Their commander stood before them, a scarred brute in chainmail, hefting a battle-axe as if it weighed nothing.

He grinned when he saw Kael step forward, his laugh like gravel grinding together.
"You think to defy Lord Malrik? You'll die screaming, boy. Just like your precious king."

Kael froze. His heart stuttered. The words, the mocking boast of Malrik's hound, cut deeper than steel.

But rage rose quickly, burning away doubt.

Kael stepped forward, sword raised, eyes blazing.
"Then let me show you what it means to fight for Elaria."

The brute roared and charged.

The clash was thunder.

The axe came down like a hammer, the impact rattling Kael's bones as he caught it on his blade. Sparks burst. His arms shook violently, nearly buckling.

Too strong.

He twisted aside just in time as the axe carved into the dirt, leaving a crater. He slashed, but the brute's armor caught the blow.
"Little kid," the man jeered, shoving him back. "I'll split you from crown to groin."

Kael's mind raced. He could not match the man's strength. But he did not have to.

Lyra's arrows sang through the smoke, striking the commander's side and slowing him. Thorne struck from behind, his blade slicing deep into the man's thigh.

The brute roared in pain, staggering.

Kael saw his chance. He lunged, driving his sword into the gap beneath the chainmail. His blade sank deep.

The commander gasped, blood bubbling from his lips. His axe slipped from his grip and crashed to the earth. He fell, face twisted in shock as the firelight painted him red and gold.

Kael stood over him, chest heaving. The battle was done.

Morning light brought silence.

The village smoldered, scarred but standing. The survivors gathered in the square, hollow-eyed but alive. They bowed their heads to Kael, not knowing who he truly was, only that he had fought for them when no one else would.

Kael's stomach churned under their gratitude. He was not ready for this, for their hope or their weight. But he could not turn away either.

As they walked the road out of the valley, Kael was quiet. The screams, the fire, the commander's mocking voice, all of it gnawed at him.

Finally, he spoke.
"We cannot do this alone. Against a handful, maybe. But Malrik commands armies. We need more than a sword, a bow, and a knight. We need strength. Someone who can change the tide of a battle just by standing in it."

Thorne's lips curved into something like a grim smile.
"I may know just the one."

Kael glanced at him.
"Who?"

"In Blackbridge," Thorne said, voice low. "Whispers speak of an orc. A brute larger than any man, the sole survivor of a slaughtered clan. They call him Brutus. In the underground, he is half legend, half nightmare. If he can be convinced, he could be what you seek."

Lyra raised an eyebrow.
"And if he cannot?"

Thorne's smile faded.
"Then he will be a problem."

Kael looked ahead to the horizon where smoke still rose faintly behind them. His hands ached from the fight, but deeper still, his soul ached from the truth of it: they were too few.

He drew a breath.
"Then we find him."

Lyra gave a short nod, her lips tightening as if she already foresaw trouble.

“Blackbridge awaits,” Thorne muttered, his voice rough as gravel. Then he shook his head. “But not for me.”

Kael frowned.
“What do you mean?”

Thorne’s gaze shifted from the road to him, and for a heartbeat Kael saw something he rarely caught in his mentor’s eye: pride, tempered with quiet sorrow.

“You do not need me to bloody every blade for you,” Thorne said. “Not anymore. You have allies now. You have a voice. And Blackbridge is the place where you need to prove it without me standing in the way.”

Kael’s hand tightened around the hilt of his sword.
“You think I’m ready to face it alone?”

“I think,” Thorne growled, “that the boy I saved and raised in shadows is gone. What stands here now is a man, one who must be seen as a leader in his own right. If I march into Blackbridge at your side, they will see the Butcher of Irondeep, not Kael. Not their rightful king. Do you understand?”

The words struck deeper than any blade could have. Kael felt both the weight of them and the sting of doubt pressing against his chest. But beneath it was a strange warmth, a trust so rare from Thorne it almost startled him.

“Then where will you go?” Kael asked quietly.

Thorne turned back to the road, his eye narrowing as though he saw something far beyond the horizon.
“Emberdeep. There is a place there, a safehouse hidden long before Malrik’s reign. Old friends of your father’s still linger in

those streets, if rumor holds true. If there are answers to be found, truths Malrik tried to bury, they will be there. I will wait for you in Emberdeep, Kael. You bring them hope in Blackbridge, and I will make certain we have a haven waiting when you return."

Kael swallowed, nodding slowly.
"And if you're wrong?"

Thorne's scarred mouth curved into something that was almost a smile.
"Then I will burn Emberdeep to its bones and start again."

It was the closest thing to reassurance the old general would ever give.

Kael wanted to argue, wanted to insist Thorne stay. But deep down, he knew the man was right. The time for shadows was ending. If he meant to stand against Malrik, the world had to see him, not just as the son of a dead king, but as Kael himself.

Thorne rested one massive hand on his shoulder. The grip was steady, iron strong, grounding him.

"You're ready for this," Thorne said, softer now, almost like a father to a son. "More than you think. Do not waste it."

Then he released him, turned, and walked back toward the campfire without another word.

Kael stood on the road a long time after, staring toward Blackbridge, his heart heavy and fierce all at once.

For the first time, he would lead without Thorne at his side.
And that thought terrified him.

But it also lit a fire in his chest that would not be put out.

Chapter 6 - Blackbridge

The city of Blackbridge was the kind of place people entered when they had nothing left to lose.

Tucked beneath jagged cliffs on Elaria's southern border, the settlement had begun as a dwarven outpost, all cut stone and solid bridges, a place meant to endure. But the dwarves were long gone. What remained had been twisted into something else entirely. Smugglers took the old tunnels, slavers filled the markets, and exiled warlords carved out territory in the shadows. Now the city breathed vice the way other places breathed air.

Its lower levels throbbed with noise: the clang of coins, the growl of wagers, the shouts of merchants peddling venom-laced wine and knives chipped with rust. The smell was a churning tide of blood, smoke, and rot, cut through with the faint tang of brine from the river mouth.

Kael kept his hood low as he and Lyra slipped through the crowd. Even hidden, he felt out of place. His whole life had been forest paths, mountain ridges, and the quiet of firelight and steel practice under Thorne's eye. Here, every step felt like sinking into a swamp of strangers.

"Eyes forward," Lyra murmured beside him, her voice soft as silk. "You look like a lost fawn."

"I feel like one," Kael muttered.

She smirked, adjusting the strap of her bow across her shoulder. "Blackbridge eats lost things. Better to look like a wolf."

Kael straightened, keeping his stride purposeful. It was difficult when every glance he caught in the torchlight looked hungry.

The pit's roar reached them before the doors. A low thunder of voices rising, boots stomping, coins clinking against stone. The building itself was a repurposed dwarven hall, pillars carved with runes that had long since been defaced by knives and paint.

The central chamber opened like a wound in the floor, a sunken ring where fighters bled for coin.

Kael and Lyra pressed to the railing with the others.

The walls of the arena were slick with damp, iron bars forming gates at either end. Torches lined the pit like the teeth of some colossal beast, each flame guttering in rhythm with the chants of the crowd.

The fighters below were monsters. Not in name alone. Chained ogres, tattooed berserkers, half-mad sellswords whose eyes were glazed with powder and fury. They swung weapons dulled from overuse, their roars lost beneath the hunger of those above.

One name cut louder than the rest.

"Bru-tus! Bru-tus! Bru-tus!"

The chant shook the walls, boots hammering the stone floor in unison. Coins flew in arcs of bronze and silver. Wine spilled from mugs as men shouted odds, some grinning with rotten teeth, others already clawing over their purses.

Kael leaned over the railing just in time to see the next challenger stumble through the far gate.

An ogre. But not like any Kael had seen.

This one bore two heads, each gnashing teeth and screaming curses. Twin hammers hung from its fists, each as wide as a human chest, Chains rattled as it pulled free from handlers too afraid to step close.

The crowd went wild.

From the opposite gate came the orc. Brutus.

He was a mountain of green muscle, his tusks glinting in the torchlight. Scars traced his body in crude maps of violence, every line a story. Shackles hung loose on his wrists, not because he was captive, but because the pit masters knew no other iron could hold him. His only weapon was his body, and it was more than enough.

The ogre roared and charged.

Kael tensed, hand twitching toward his sword. He could feel the weight of the moment, the inevitability of collision.

Brutus did not move. Not at first. He stood with an almost casual stillness, head tilted, shoulders loose, as though bored. Then, at the last heartbeat, he shifted.

The first hammer whistled down. Brutus stepped aside, caught the ogre's wrist in both hands, and twisted.

Snap.

The sound cracked louder than the roar. One of the ogre's heads shrieked in fury, the other in pain.

Before the beast could recover, Brutus drove his fist into its gut. Once. Twice. A third blow like a boulder hurled from the heavens. The ogre collapsed, breathless, hammers dropping from limp fingers.

The crowd erupted.

Kael blinked, stunned. He had expected brutality, but there was grace to it as well. Speed no one his size should have. Control born of endless battles.

Beside him, Lyra chewed on a skewer of roasted lizard meat she had bought from a vendor, utterly calm.

"That him?"

Kael nodded. "That's him."

She smirked faintly. "Looks like a charmer."

The fight was not over. Another gate opened. This time a chained dire wolf was loosed, fur patchy from mistreatment, eyes burning with starvation. The crowd howled as the beast leapt straight for the orc.

Brutus turned, caught the wolf by the throat mid-air, and slammed it into the ground with such force the stone cracked beneath it. He did not kill it. Instead, he pinned it, eyes locking on the handlers above until they dragged it back with hooked chains.

The chant turned fevered.

"BRU-TUS! BRU-TUS!"

Kael swallowed hard. "He doesn't fight like a prisoner."

"No," Lyra agreed, flicking the last of her skewer aside. "He fights like someone who chooses to be here."

Kael's boots scraped along the stone steps as he and Lyra descended after the match, slipping past drunk gamblers and distracted guards. Torchlight flickered along iron bars, casting jagged shadows across chained men and women. Some stared hollow-eyed, others sharpened crude blades, waiting for their next summons to bleed.

They reached Cell Seven.

Brutus sat cross-legged on the floor, a broken spearhead balanced on his palm as if it were a toy. His tusks gleamed faintly when he saw them.

“You lost, human?”

Kael stepped closer. “I’m here to offer you something.”

Brutus snorted, his voice deep enough to vibrate the bars. “Let me guess. Freedom. Justice. A noble quest to save the kingdom.”

Kael did not flinch. “Something like that.”

Brutus chuckled, the sound a rolling growl, amused and bitter. “I’ve heard better lines from slavers. What makes you think I want out?”

Kael leaned forward, lowering his voice. “Because I know you are the last of your clan. And I know you want more than this pit. You want to fight for something that matters, something that would make your clan proud.”

The orc’s grin faltered. His eyes, dark and sharp, studied Kael for a long, heavy moment.

“You’ve got guts, boy,” Brutus muttered. “But information won’t open these bars.”

Kael nodded once and stepped aside.

Lyra dropped from the rafters above, landing silent as falling ash. She tossed a ring of keys through the bars. They clattered on the floor.

Brutus stared. "You two are either idiots or desperate."

"We're both," Kael said. "But we're also building something. And we need a hammer."

The orc rose slowly. His size filled the cell, his shoulders nearly brushing the ceiling. He picked up the keys, weighed them in his hand, then looked Kael dead in the eye.

"You know what happens when I walk out of this cell?"

Kael held his gaze. "You start fighting for something real."

Brutus's tusks gleamed as his grin returned. "Wrong."

He unlocked the door and shoved it open with a crash.

"I start breaking things."

The alarm bell clanged two floors above. Guards shouted, boots pounding along the walkways.

Brutus moved first, barreling through the oncoming soldiers like a storm given flesh. Shields splintered, swords flew from shattered hands, men screamed as they were tossed into walls with bone-breaking force.

Lyra's arrows whistled through the chaos, each one finding a knee, a shoulder, a hand. She did not waste kills. She carved gaps for them to move through.

Kael cut down stragglers who got too close, his blade flashing in the torchlight. Every clash echoed in the narrow halls.

"Left!" Lyra called, and Kael followed without hesitation.

They reached the sewer grate. Brutus tore it open with a single pull. It flew clean off its hinges, clattering into the dark beyond.

They climbed into the night air, the stench of the pit giving way to the sharp bite of the river wind. Behind them, shouts still rang, but the city swallowed the noise as they vanished into twisting alleys.

Later, by the fire outside the city walls, Brutus tossed a log into the flames. Sparks leapt high, painting his tusks in gold.

"So let me get this straight," he rumbled. "You're the last royal, raised in the woods, training for vengeance. Elf with the deadpan stare is your scout. And now you want to overthrow a tyrant."

Kael met his gaze. "That about sums it up."

Brutus smirked, shaking his head. "You're all insane."

Lyra sipped from her cup of bitter tea, utterly calm. "You just punched a two-headed ogre unconscious."

Brutus lifted a finger. "A two-headed ogre."

Kael smiled faintly. "You in or not?"

For a moment, Brutus stared into the flames. The crackle filled the silence, painting his face in shadow and light. Then he leaned back, his grin spreading wide.

"I'm in."

And just like that, the broken pieces began to come together.

Chapter 7 - Echoes Beneath the Stone

The ruins of Var'Lath stood like the broken teeth of a dead god.

Once an elven stronghold, the centuries had left it nothing but crumbling archways and shattered towers, half swallowed by the earth and strangled with vines. Mist clung to the ground, and the evening air felt heavy, as if it carried whispers of old blood.

Kael studied the map one last time.
"This is the place," he said, rolling it up. "The merchant said his caravan was ambushed near here. Whatever they stole was dragged into the ruins."

Lyra's sharp gaze swept the overgrown courtyard. "Or whoever. You sure this isn't a trap?"

"Everything's a trap," Brutus rumbled, adjusting the massive great axe over his back. "The question is who's dumb enough to set one for us."

Kael smiled faintly. "Let's find out."

The entrance was a yawning mouth of stone, half collapsed and slick with moss. They descended slowly, torchlight flickering against walls etched with faded runes. The air was colder here, damp with a strange metallic tang.

Lyra's voice was soft but edged with warning. "This place doesn't feel empty."

Brutus cracked his knuckles. "Good. I was getting bored."

Kael crouched near a half-buried statue, an elven warrior holding a curved blade. The carvings were almost alive, worn

yet still beautiful.
“These ruins are older than Elaria. Older than the kingdom itself.”

Lyra’s eyes lingered on the runes. “They say Var’Lath fell when its people angered the spirits of the deepwood.”

Kael stood, gripping his sword. “Then let’s hope they’ve forgiven us.”

The first sign of danger was the sound, a faint skittering like claws scraping stone.

Kael raised a hand. “Hear that?”

Brutus swung his torch toward the shadows. “Hear what”

Screeeee!

The walls seemed to explode as pale shapes leapt from the dark. Chitinous bodies. Multiple limbs. Faces like twisted masks of bone.

Skarrin.

Lyra loosed two arrows in rapid succession, each one striking true into the creature’s eye socket. “Of course it’s giant corpse-eaters. Why wouldn’t it be?”

Kael spun, parrying one with his sword before driving his dagger between its mandibles. Brutus simply grabbed one by the neck and slammed it against the wall until its body cracked like brittle armor.

But for each they cut down, two more emerged.

“They’re guarding something,” Kael shouted. “Keep moving forward!”

They burst into a wide underground hall, the ceiling high and ribbed with roots. A stone dais stood at the center, upon which sat a sealed chest, iron bound and pulsing faintly with blue light.

Kael felt his stomach drop.

“That’s not just stolen cargo,” he muttered.

The skarrin swarmed closer, a wall of claws and teeth.

Lyra backed toward the dais, firing arrow after arrow. “Whatever’s in that chest better be worth it, Kael!”

Brutus grabbed the chest’s lid and pulled. It did not budge. “It’s sealed!”

“Then break it!” Kael shouted.

Brutus grinned.
“Finally, something I’m good at.”

He raised his axe and brought it down with a single earth-shaking strike. The lock shattered.

The light inside spilled out, washing over the chamber like a breath of fire. Kael froze.

Inside the chest was not gold, nor weapons, but a crystal shard, smooth and jagged, glowing with a heartbeat of its own. Strange glyphs coiled across its surface like living flame.

“What is that?” Lyra whispered.

Kael reached toward it.

The instant his fingers brushed the crystal, the chamber shook. The walls trembled. The skarrin screeched and retreated as though burned.

And then, a voice.

"Blood of flame. Heir of the crown. You have awakened me."

Kael's mind went white-hot. Images flashed: dragons soaring over mountains, a burning throne, a figure in chains screaming in defiance.

He stumbled back, clutching his head.

Lyra grabbed him by the shoulders. "Kael, what's happening?"

Brutus looked around as cracks formed in the floor. "We're leaving. Now."

They ran.

The ruins groaned as stone pillars toppled. The skarrin fled in all directions, their screeches fading into the distance. Kael felt the crystal pulsing against his palm as though it were alive, whispering in a language older than the stars.

They burst into the night just as the entrance caved in behind them, sealing the ruin once more.

Kael collapsed onto the grass, chest heaving.

Lyra knelt down beside him. "You want to tell us what just happened?"

Kael looked at the crystal in his hand. Its light dimmed, but its warmth remained.

"I don't know," he said quietly. "But whatever this is, it was waiting for me."

Brutus gnawed on a roasted rabbit leg while staring at the crystal. "That thing's cursed. You can smell it."

Lyra nodded. "He's right. It feels wrong. Or maybe too right. Like it's meant for you."

Kael stared at the flickering light.

When he closed his eyes, he heard the voice again.

"Bloodfire."

The word sent chills down his spine.

Chapter 8 - Fire and Shadows

The night after their escape from the ruins, the forest was too quiet.

No owls. No wind. Not even the whisper of leaves. Kael sat by the fire, the crystal shard resting on a flat stone in front of him. Its faint blue light pulsed like a heartbeat, casting eerie shadows on their faces.

Brutus spat a bone into the flames. "That thing's watching us."

Lyra adjusted her bowstring, her tone sharp. "It's not watching. It's calling something. I can feel it."

Kael did not respond. His hand hovered over the shard, a strange warmth crawling up his arm when he touched it. It was not just power. It was familiar, as if something deep in his blood recognized it.

Then the forest split with a voice.

"Step away from that shard, boy, if you want to live."

Kael and Lyra sprang to their feet instantly, weapons drawn. Brutus cracked his neck, already grinning like a wolf about to fight.

A figure emerged from the tree line, tall, slender, and wreathed in faint violet glow. Her cloak was tattered, and beneath it, the faint outline of dark, clawed markings ran down her pale arms. Her eyes glowed violet in the firelight.

She was beautiful, but dangerous.

"Who are you?" Kael demanded.

The woman ignored the question, her gaze fixed on the shard. "Give it to me."

Lyra scoffed. "Not likely."

The woman sighed, exasperated. "Then I'll take it."

She raised a hand, and the world erupted in fire.

The ground beneath Kael's feet split, jagged lines glowing like molten rock. A blast of purple flame roared toward them, throwing Brutus backward and forcing Lyra to dive behind a log. Kael barely had time to raise his sword, the fire swirling around the blade like a living storm.

"Magic," Brutus grunted from the dirt. "I hate magic."

The woman stepped closer, her expression pained rather than angry. "I don't want to hurt you. But you cannot hold that shard. It will tear you apart."

Kael tightened his grip on his sword. "You will have to trust me, because I'm not letting it go."

The woman's control faltered. The flames flickered violently, the ground cracking as if the forest itself trembled. Lyra loosed an arrow that disintegrated in midair, caught by a surge of unstable energy.

"Kael!" Lyra shouted, ducking another blast. "She can't control it. She'll burn us all."

Kael stepped forward, sword raised, and locked eyes with the woman. Something in her gaze shifted, like a flicker of recognition.

"Your blood," she whispered. "You're… no. It cannot be."

Kael frowned. "What do you know about me?"

Before she could answer, another pulse of magic erupted from her body, sending everyone sprawling. Kael hit the ground hard, but as the flames rushed toward him, something inside him snapped.

His hand ignited.

Not with her violet fire, but with **Bloodfire**. Crimson, fierce, and alive.

The woman's eyes widened. "You… you carry it."

Kael did not know what she meant. But the Bloodfire flared, meeting her magic in a violent clash that split the night sky. Trees caught fire. The ground scorched black.

Brutus grabbed Lyra and pulled her clear as Kael and the woman's magic collided in a blinding storm of red and purple.

When the flames finally died, Kael was on his knees, panting. His sword still smoked with red heat, and the shard beside him pulsed wildly, as if it recognized what had happened.

The woman collapsed across from him, her breathing ragged. The demonic markings on her arms faded slightly, leaving pale skin beneath.

Lyra approached cautiously, bow drawn. "Who the hell are you?"

The woman looked up, her voice hoarse. "Thalia."

Kael raised an eyebrow. "And why do you want this shard?"

"Because it is one of the Crown shards. Pieces of the old Dragonfire Crown. They are bound to the blood kings, and if you are not careful, they will kill you before Malrik does."

Kael exchanged a glance with Lyra.

Brutus groaned as he sat up. "So, we're keeping her, then?"

Later that night, after the chaos had settled, Thalia sat with her back against a log, avoiding everyone's gaze. Her fingers trembled as she traced glowing sigils in the dirt, trying to bleed off excess magic.

Kael approached her. "You almost killed us."

She smirked faintly. "I didn't mean to."

"Do you always lose control like that?"

Her eyes darkened. "When I'm around things that amplify me. The shard, your blood… it pulls at me."

Kael sat down across from her. "You know things about Malrik. About this crown. We could use that."

Thalia laughed bitterly. "You don't use someone like me. I'm not stable. Half my magic is demon-born. The other half wants to consume me."

"Then maybe you need something to fight for," Kael said quietly.

She looked at him, really looked. And for a moment, her fire dimmed.

Chapter 9 - Blades in the Dark

The wind whispered low through the trees, rustling leaves that had long turned brittle with the approach of autumn. The forest was quiet, too quiet.

Kael led the way, sword drawn but lowered, eyes scanning the narrow deer path ahead. Behind him, Lyra moved like a shadow, bow ready. Brutus brought up the rear, massive arms tensed, his great axe strapped across his back. Thalia walked off to the side, glancing over her shoulder now and then, violet eyes shimmering faintly with unease.

Their mercenary contact was supposed to meet them hours ago.

"Something's wrong," Lyra muttered. "This route is usually active. Hunters. Traders. We have seen no one since dawn."

Brutus snorted. "Orcs call this kind of silence a death song."

Kael raised a hand to stop them. "Then stay sharp. We fall back to the glade if anything happens."

Before they could move another step, the air shifted. Cold and sudden. Kael's breath frosted. A thin mist curled at his feet.

Then whispers.

From the trees. From the air. From within their own ears.

Thalia's eyes flared. "Wards. Shadow-bent ones. We are walking into a trap."

The first strike came fast, a glint of obsidian slicing through the air. Kael ducked, parried the second blow, and shouted, "Ambush!"

From all sides, black-robed figures emerged. Malrik's shadow assassins, silent and swift. Their faces were hidden behind bone masks, their blades curved and coated in thick, gleaming venom.

Brutus roared and charged, swinging wide and cleaving two assassins clean in half. Lyra loosed a volley of arrows, her movements calm and precise, each shot finding its mark. But they kept coming.

Thalia raised her hand. Magic pulsed in jagged violet arcs, slamming into the enemies, but her control slipped. Energy cracked trees and scorched the ground near Kael.

"THALIA, FOCUS!" Kael shouted.

"I am trying," she gasped.

One of the assassins slipped past the others and lunged toward her, blade raised.

Kael did not hesitate. He launched forward, intercepted the strike, and disarmed the attacker in one fluid motion. "We do this together, remember?"

She nodded, biting her lip, and this time, when she cast, the magic was cleaner and controlled.

Still, they were being driven back, herded toward a cliff's edge just beyond the tree line.

"We are not going to outlast them like this," Lyra called out. "They are driving us."

Kael looked at each of them, then at the mist-shrouded battlefield. His heartbeat slowed. A strange clarity took hold.

“Then we stop running,” he said, raising his sword. “Form around me. We turn their trap against them.”

Brutus looked at him, surprised. “You got a plan, pup?”

Kael nodded. “I will draw their fire. Lyra, cover us from the ridge. Thalia, when I give the word, drop every ounce of flame you have behind them. Brutus, keep anything off my back.”

Brutus grinned. “Now that I can do.”

They moved fast. Lyra sprinted to higher ground, blending with the trees. Brutus followed Kael, who strode into the open like bait, sword raised. Thalia hung back, eyes glowing brighter with coiled, unstable energy.

The assassins surged forward, too confident.

“Now!” Kael shouted.

Flames burst behind the assassins as Thalia unleashed her power. The shadows broke formation, and Brutus barreled through the chaos like a wrecking ball, sending them scattering.

Kael’s sword flashed in the firelight, cutting down one after another, his movements clean and purposeful. He was not just fighting now. He was leading.

And they followed.

When the dust settled, the last of the assassins fled into the woods. The silence returned, this time earned.

Kael sheathed his sword. “Everyone okay?”

Thalia leaned on her knees, breathless but smiling. “You… really are your father’s son.”

Lyra stepped down from the ridge, nodding. "I was not sure you could lead. Now I am starting to believe."

Brutus gave him a hard slap on the back. "Not bad, pup. Not bad at all."

Kael looked at them, his mismatched band of allies now a true unit. "This was just the beginning," he said, eyes narrowing. "Malrik will not stop until we make him."

The fire crackled as night settled once more. But now, there was warmth beneath the silence. A spark of unity. Of purpose. Of hope.

They sat close to the flames, the smell of ash and blood still clinging to their clothes. Thalia had fallen quiet, her hands trembling faintly as she pressed herbs against her burns. Lyra sat sharpening her arrows, her gaze flicking now and then toward Kael with a trace of something softer than usual.

Brutus, though, just stared at Kael across the fire, his expression unreadable in the shifting glow.

Finally, the big man leaned forward, voice low but steady. "I have fought beside a lot of men, Kael. Seen leaders who talk big, and kings who wear crowns they did not earn. But tonight…" He paused, nodding once. "…tonight, I saw something different."

Kael frowned slightly, unsure how to answer. "Different how?"

Brutus reached for the haft of his axe, running a calloused hand down the scarred wood. "You do not fight for glory. Or for fear. You fight because you have to, for them." He jerked his chin toward Lyra and Thalia. "For all of us."

The silence deepened. Even the forest seemed to hold its breath.

Then Brutus met Kael's eyes without wavering. "So, hear me now, pup. From this day forward, I will be your shield. When the time comes to take back your throne, I will be at your side, axe in hand, no matter the cost. That is my promise."

The words landed heavier than Kael expected. His throat tightened, but he managed a small, solemn nod. "Then I will hold you to it, Brutus."

The big man grinned, teeth flashing in the firelight. "Good. Would not have it any other way."

The flame popped and hissed, sending sparks into the night sky. Around the fire, the four of them sat in rare silence, not as wanderers thrown together by chance, but as comrades bound by blood and promise.

Kael gazed into the fire, feeling the weight of Brutus's vow settle into his bones like iron. It was no longer just his fight.

It was theirs.

Interlude - A King of Shadows

The air in the throne chamber was cold, unnaturally still. The torches along the blackstone walls burned with green flame, enchanted to flicker soundlessly and cast long, dancing shadows across the obsidian floor.

Lord Malrik sat motionless upon the onyx throne, one leg folded over the other, fingertips steepled. The black crown atop his head glinted faintly in the firelight, but the true authority lay in his eyes, ice pale and utterly devoid of warmth.

Before him, one of the shadow assassins knelt, trembling. Blood seeped from a gash across his arm where Kael's sword had caught him.

"You let them escape," Malrik said, voice as soft as a whisper, yet it echoed through the chamber like a bell toll.

"My lord," the assassin rasped. "We underestimated the boy. He fought like... like..."

"Like Thorne," Malrik finished for him. He stood, slowly descending the obsidian steps. "You were given numbers, poison, the gift of silence and surprise, and still you failed to kill a half-trained prince and his mismatch band of vagabonds."

The assassin bowed lower. "I accept whatever punishment you deem..."

"You misunderstand," Malrik said gently. "This is not punishment."

He flicked his finger. The assassin's body convulsed. Shadow tendrils burst from beneath his skin, wrapping around his throat and limbs. His scream was swallowed whole as he was dragged into the floor and vanished into the black stone without a trace.

Silence returned.

From the shadows behind the throne, General Veska emerged, her robes a cascade of smoke, her face half hidden by a mask of bone and shadowsteel.

“He’s growing stronger,” she said. “More confident. That strike formation was Thorne's. He is remembering.”

Malrik turned to her, the calm mask on his face slipping slightly into a scowl. “Then we must accelerate the plan.”

Veska tilted her head. “Shall I send the next wave? The Blood Crows?”

“No,” Malrik replied. “Let him taste victory. Let him gather allies and think he has hope.”

He stepped to the wide window behind the throne, watching the mist crawl over Elaria like a shroud. “Let them hope,” Malrik murmured, lips curving into a thin smile. “The higher they reach for the light, the harder it is when I drag them back into the dark.”

He traced a finger along the cold glass. “When the boy reaches the ruins at Virestone,” Malrik continued, “send the Wraithborn. I want him broken.”

He paused, then added quietly, “And Veska, next time, do not bring me failure dressed as a report. Bring me his blade. Or his bones.”

Chapter 10 - Horns of the Mengok

The tavern smelled of spiced meat and old ale, its hearth crackling against the cool night beyond its wooden walls. Kael sat hunched forward at a small, scarred table, his companions gathered close. Lyra leaned back with her arms crossed, eyes darting toward the corners of the room as though measuring every shadow. Brutus tore into a loaf of bread as if it had wronged him, crumbs dusting his tusk. Thalia sat quietly, her black hair catching the firelight as she toyed absently with the rim of her cup.

The four of them had been traveling for days, the dust of the roads still clinging to their boots, and the tavern offered a rare respite. Yet the air was thick not only with smoke and laughter but with whispers. Kael could feel the eyes on them.

"Heroes," one man muttered in a low voice, barely audible over the hum. "Or trouble, depending on who you ask."

"They say that's the prince," another voice whispered from across the room, low and urgent.

A man snorted into his mug. "The prince? Don't be a fool. He would have died the night the king and queen were cut down. Everyone knows they gave their lives protecting Elaria. No one survived that fire."

"Still," the first insisted, "look at him. The way he carries himself... the sword at his side. Doesn't that look like royal blood to you?"

"Looks like trouble," the second replied. "Keep your tongue behind your teeth before it gets cut out."

Kael clenched his jaw but kept his gaze on the table. He had grown used to whispers, half reverent and half suspicious. Lyra had already caught the source. She leaned forward, lips curling in a smirk.

"Seems you're the talk of the kingdom already, boy." Her voice was teasing, but something watchful lay beneath it.

Before Kael could answer, the tone of the room shifted. A group of travelers nearby spoke not of politics, or rumor, but of something darker.

"... adventurers, all torn apart," one man said in a hushed tone, hands trembling around his mug. "Said it moved like a shadow, taller than any man, with horns like an elk and claws sharper than a direfang."

"Aye, I heard the same," another added. "A thing of bark and bone. Looks like a tree come to life, only worse. They say it haunts the woods north of here and takes men in the night."

Kael's head lifted, the firelight catching in his eyes as he whispered the name he had heard only in stories.

"A Mengok."

Lyra arched a brow. "What is it?"

Kael exhaled slowly. "I've never seen one. But Thorne told me stories. My father fought them once, near the forests at the edge of Elaria City. Creatures cursed by shadow and flame. Not natural. Not alive in the way trees are alive."

Brutus tore another chunk of bread and grunted. "Horns, claws, bark. Doesn't sound so bad. I've split worse."

“Don’t be so sure,” Kael replied. “They say a Mengok can only be killed if its horns are severed and burned. Otherwise, it rises again, no matter how deep the wounds.”

A silence lingered until the waitress approached with a pitcher. Kael stopped her with a raised hand.

“You’ve heard the talk,” he said gently. “About this creature.”

The young woman’s face paled, and she gripped the pitcher tighter. “Everyone's heard. Adventurers think themselves bold, but none return. People are scared. If the thing keeps hunting, it won't stop at wanderers. It’ll come here.”

“Where was it last seen?” Kael asked.

She shook her head quickly. “I don’t know. No one does. We just pray the stories don't bring it closer.”

From a table near the back, an older man with clouded eyes spoke. “North,” he rasped. “Near the hollow clearing where the wind always howls. Folks say it drags its kills there.”

Kael nodded in thanks and turned to his companions. His voice dropped into something steady and commanding. “We go tonight.”

Brutus grinned wide and slammed his fist on the table. “Finally. Some real fun.”

Lyra rolled her eyes, but her hand was already reaching for her bow. “If you call being gutted fun, then yes. Let’s hunt.”

Thalia remained quiet, her gaze sliding to Kael as though weighing his conviction.

The forest loomed before them, cloaked in mist. The moon broke through the canopy in silver shards, and every breath carried the weight of damp earth and rot. Kael led the way, his sword strapped tight at his hip, his hand brushing the hilt for reassurance.

The wind whispered through the trees, a constant, eerie rustling that seemed almost like words.

“This place feels wrong,” Thalia murmured, pulling her cloak tighter. “Like the trees are speaking.”

Brutus chuckled. “What are they saying? Run away, little girl, before the orc eats all your bread?”

Thalia’s lips twitched into a smile despite herself.

Kael’s eyes scanned the canopy. He felt it before he saw it, the oppressive presence watching them. Lyra felt it too. She drew an arrow and whispered, “It’s here.”

“I know,” Kael said, tightening his grip on his sword.

The silence deepened. Then, with a groan of wood and a hiss of wind, something massive shifted above them.

The Mengok dropped from the treetops like a nightmare. Its body was twisted bark and sinew, claws sharp as obsidian, horns branching wide and jagged. Its eyes burned with a sickly green glow, and across its tree barked chest were black sigils of Malrik’s design.

Kael’s stomach tightened. Malrik’s corruption reached even here.

The Mengok lunged. Claws slashed with brutal precision, forcing them to scatter. Brutus met its charge head-on, swinging his axe with a roar. The blow cracked across the creature's side, sending shards of bark flying, but it barely slowed.

“The horns,” Kael shouted. “Sever and burn them. It’s the only way.”

Lyra released an arrow, the shaft sinking into the creature’s shoulder. It twisted toward her, shrieking. Kael intercepted its next strike, though the claws raked against his guard and nearly knocked him off his feet.

Brutus grabbed one of its twisted arms and heaved, slamming it into a tree. The impact split bark and sent leaves falling, but the creature rose again, eyes locked on Kael.

Kael darted forward, his blade flashed in the moonlight. With a fierce cry, he struck and cleaved through one massive horn. The Mengok screamed, a sound like splintering wood mixed with human agony.

It lunged with terrifying speed. Claws aimed for Kael’s chest.

“Kael!” Lyra’s voice cut through the night. An arrow struck the creature’s wrist, forcing its aim wide. The claws grazed Kael’s shoulder instead of piercing through. Pain flared, but he stayed upright.

Brutus seized the opening. With a roar, he swung his axe and severed the second horn cleanly.

The Mengok shrieked, its body trembling as cracks raced through its bark-like skin.

“Now,” Kael shouted. “Thalia, burn them.”

Thalia stepped forward, eyes blazing. She summoned fire that licked across her palms, then cast it onto the severed horns. Flames roared to life, engulfing the twisted bone. The Mengok thrashed, its form igniting. Moments later it collapsed into ash, scattered by the wind.

Silence settled over the group. Kael lowered his blade, sweat and blood streaking his brow. “It bore Malrik’s mark. Even the wild is twisted by him now.”

Lyra wiped blood from her cheek. “Then the kingdom is worse off than we thought.”

Brutus spat into the ashes, still grinning. “Whatever it was, it’s dead now. You’re welcome.”

Even Lyra let a brief laugh escape.

The tavern was quieter when they returned, though every head turned as they stepped inside. Their boots were stained with mud and ash, and Kael’s arm still bled from the Mengok’s strike.

The same waitress approached, wide-eyed. “You... you came back.”

Kael nodded. “It’s done. You don't need to fear the forest anymore. The creature is gone.”

She gasped, disbelief warring with relief. “How? Who are you?”

Kael glanced at his companions, then back to her. His voice held no boast.

“Just a group,” he said quietly, “that plans to change this kingdom.”

The tavern fell silent. When whispers rose again, they carried a new tone. Not doubt. Hope.

Kael felt the weight settle on his shoulders. Leadership was no longer a choice. It was a mantle he could not set down.

Chapter 11 - Echoes Beneath Virestone

The wind howled through the jagged peaks surrounding the Virestone ruins, a bitter chill clinging to every stone. Moss and frost laced the crumbling towers, once a proud fortress of the First Kings, now just bones of a bygone age.

Kael stood at the edge of the ruined courtyard, his breath steaming in the air. The ground beneath their feet pulsed faintly, as if the land itself remembered the blood spilled here. His fingers tightened around the hilt of his sword.

"So, this is Virestone," Lyra murmured, drawing her cloak tighter. Her eyes scanned the ancient carvings. "These walls were built long before the kingdom fell. There is magic etched in them, old bitter magic."

Brutus grunted, sniffing the air. "I smell rot. Not normal rot. Something that shouldn't be."

Thalia knelt near a cracked pillar, her fingers glowing faintly with unstable magic as she touched the stone. "This place hums with echoes. Whatever is buried here does not want us near."

Kael said nothing. The closer they got, the more the voices whispered. They were not words, just sensations. Rage. Hunger. Mourning.

They stepped deeper into the ruins.

Hidden beneath the fortress, a spiral stair descended into darkness. Lyra lit a crystal with her magic, casting pale blue light that danced across murals and ancient runes. The path led them to a massive circular chamber.

At its center stood a monolith of black stone, veined with glowing red sigils. Malrik's mark.

"That is it," Thalia whispered, stepping closer. "The heart of the curse. He bound something here."

Suddenly, the air shifted.

A low, wet breath echoed across the chamber, and the shadows stirred. From the base of the monolith, the **Wraithborn** rose.

A towering figure, wrapped in tattered ghost light and dripping darkness like tar. Its face was a hollow mask, and its voice was many, all screaming at once.

"You carry his blood. His light. You do not belong."

Kael stepped forward. "I am not my father."

The Wraithborn howled, and the sound tore through their minds like knives. Its arms stretched unnaturally, forming blades of shadow. The floor cracked beneath it as it lunged.

Brutus met the creature's charge with a roar, his massive axe colliding with the shadow-forged blade. Sparks flew. Lyra shouted a spell, bolts of arcane frost striking the wraith's limbs. They passed through it like mist, but the magic slowed it.

Kael ducked low, slashing upward. His sword cut through part of the Wraithborn's arm, but instead of blood, black smoke spilled out, spiraling back into place.

"It is not fully in this world," Lyra cried. "We need to bind it first."

Thalia stepped forward, arms trembling. Magic flared wildly around her, unstable and brilliant.

"No," Kael shouted. "You will lose control."

"I have to try."

Her magic struck the monolith. Runes shattered, and the chamber shook.

The Wraithborn screamed, its body flickering. Shadow blades tore through the air like streaks of living darkness, each one whispering of death. Lyra moved with sharp precision, deflecting what she could, until one found its mark.

The blade struck her shoulder with a sickening thud.

"Lyra," Kael shouted, spinning toward her as she staggered, clutching the wound. "Are you alright?"

Her jaw clenched against the pain, eyes burning with determination. "I am fine. Go for the kill."

Kael's eyes hardened. He turned, voice sharp and commanding. "Brutus, distract the Wraithborn. Keep its attention on you."

Brutus nodded and charged with a battle roar.

"Thalia, lock it down with your magic. I need it contained."

As Brutus drew the creature away and Thalia's hands glowed, Kael raced forward, every step fueled by fire and resolve.

He leapt, driving the blade through the wraith's chest.

With a screech like splitting metal, the creature exploded in a burst of shadow and light. The monolith cracked in half.

Kael fell to one knee, panting. Around him, the others stood dazed, wounded but alive. Brutus spat black ichor from his mouth. "Next time, we burn the ruins first."

Lyra chuckled weakly. "Agreed."

Thalia sat on the floor, visibly shaken. "I lost control again."

Kael looked at her, not with judgment but understanding. He offered a hand. "But you did not run."

She stared at him for a moment, then took it.

As they gathered their things, Kael turned back to the shattered monolith.

The voices were gone, but the stone still pulsed faintly, veins of red light guttering out like dying embers. Among the broken shards of obsidian, something gleamed.

"Wait," Kael said, stepping closer.

Half-buried in the rubble lay a staff. Its wood was dark as night, veined with red sigils that once marked the monolith. At its crown, however, the crystal glowed with a steady violet light, pure and unwavering.

Thalia's breath caught. She moved forward slowly, almost reverently. "This belonged to one of the most powerful mages ever from Elaria. Her name was Fay. I only remember stories of her from my parents."

Lyra frowned, keeping her bow half raised. "You are sure it is not cursed?"

Thalia ignored her. Her trembling hand closed around the staff, and the moment she touched it, the wild flares of her magic stilled. The energy that had always fought her suddenly flowed, like a raging river forced into a clean channel.

Her violet eyes widened with awe. "I can feel it. It is not suppressing me; it is guiding me. Holding me steady."

Kael watched her carefully, then nodded. "Then maybe it is not just a weapon. Maybe it is a reminder. You are stronger than you think, Thalia. You just needed something to focus you."

Thalia's lips parted, but no words came. She gripped the staff tightly, her shoulders straightening. The trembling in her hands was gone.

Brutus snorted, wiping ichor from his axe. "Took almost dying to get a proper walking stick. Worth it, I guess."

Thalia let out a soft laugh, genuine and unguarded. "More than worth it."

Kael glanced once more at the shattered monolith, then turned away. Whatever Malrik had bound here was broken. But the staff in Thalia's hands meant their fight had also given them something they desperately needed.

A new strength.

Malrik had sent that thing to kill them. They had survived.

And for the first time, Kael felt something stir in his chest. Not fear but resolve. And perhaps, just beneath it, hope.

He would not be the hunted forever.

Interlude - Cracks in the Dark

The chamber was silent except for the gentle hiss of burning incense. Dark stone pillars rose like teeth around a throne forged of obsidian and bone. Shadows moved unnaturally here, lingering even when the torches danced.

Lord Malrik sat atop his throne, fingers steepled beneath his chin. His armor shimmered like liquid night, runes pulsing faintly along the edges. His eyes, pale and cold as dead stars, stared ahead without blinking.

A lone figure approached, draped in crimson and black. The hem of her cloak scraped the floor as she knelt.

General Veska, black mistress of the Umbra Legions, her face half hidden by a mask of bone and shadowsteel.

She bowed her head low. "My lord. The Wraithborn has fallen."

Malrik's fingers twitched.

"How?" The word was not shouted, but it cracked through the room like thunder.

Veska did not flinch. "Kael and his companions fought as one. The elf girl's spells disrupted the wraith's bindings. The half demon struck the heartstone. And the boy finished it."

Malrik rose slowly, the air around him shimmering with restrained fury. "He was not meant to survive Virestone."

"No, my lord."

Silence stretched. The torches dimmed as if suffocating under Malrik's presence.

He stepped down from the dais. "Each test he survives accelerates the prophecy. His strength draws others to him. He is no longer a lost heir; he is becoming a symbol."

Veska tilted her head. "Shall I send the Nightfangs?"

"No." Malrik turned, eyes narrowing toward the northern mountains beyond the high windows. "Let him walk the path a little longer. Let him believe he is gaining ground."

He raised his hand, and the shadows in the chamber twisted, forming a circle of runes.

"Prepare the next awakening. The Wraithborn was merely a sentinel. The true challenge is the shadows of Emberdeep."

Veska nodded once. "It shall be done."

As she turned to leave, Malrik whispered, almost to himself,

"Come, Kael. Show me what legacy truly means. And I shall show you what it cost to defy a god."

Chapter 12 - Embers of Trust

The forest wrapped around them in a heavy hush, the trees like ancient sentinels watching in silence. A small fire crackled in the center of their makeshift camp, its ember light casting long shadows that danced across weary faces. Kael sat nearest to the flame, his sword sheathed but close at hand, eyes reflecting the flicker of the fire as if lost in thought.

They had survived Virestone Ruins, but just barely.

Brutus grunted as he settled onto a log with a wooden tankard in hand. His green skin was smeared with ash and blood, though none of it seemed his own. "That ghost thing fought like a demon," he muttered, staring into the fire. "Didn't think it could bleed. Didn't think it could scream."

"It wasn't supposed to," Lyra said softly from across the fire, her legs drawn up under her cloak. "The Wraithborn were bound to the old world, only kept alive by what they were denied in death."

Her eyes met Kael's then. There was something different in them. A flicker of respect, and something deeper, a concern she tried to hide.

"I could feel its pain," Thalia added from the shadows. She sat slightly apart, leaning against a tree with her arms wrapped around her knees. Her violet eyes shimmered in the dark. "Its rage. You think we won, but it was chained to him. Malrik. Like the rest of them."

Brutus raised an eyebrow. "And you aren't?"

Thalia did not flinch. "I could be. Someday. If I lose control again."

Kael looked up. The image of Thalia, wild magic ripping through stone and shadow, still haunted him. But she had pulled back. For them.

"You didn't," he said. "That matters."

She stared at him a moment, uncertain, then gave the faintest nod.

Silence fell again. The flames cracked louder in its absence. Kael felt the weight of the day settle into his shoulders. His companions were strong. Deadly. But fragile in other ways. Scarred. Like him.

"Back in the ruins," he said, voice quiet, "I didn't know what to do at first. I froze."

Brutus snorted. "Could've fooled me."

Kael smiled faintly. "I didn't lead. I just reacted."

"You made the call to stand together," Lyra said. "That's more than most leaders do."

Kael turned to her. "But what if I make the wrong call next time?"

There it was, the doubt that had festered in his chest since the moment the Wraithborn screamed his name.

"I wasn't raised to command armies or lead heroes. I was raised in shadows. Taught to survive, not inspire."

"You weren't raised to do any of this," Thalia said softly, "and yet you keep doing it."

Brutus took a deep swig from his tankard. "Look, you're not perfect. None of us are. But you're the reason we're not all dead right now. That counts for something."

Lyra leaned forward, her voice gentle. "We followed you into those ruins, Kael. We will follow you again. Not because of some prophecy, but because we trust you."

Kael let the silence settle again, this time warmer than before. The firelight danced in their eyes, flickering, fragile, but alive.

He looked at them not as strangers or even allies, but as something more. A beginning.

"Then I promise," he said at last, voice firm, "I won't just fight to survive. I'll fight for you. For all of us. And one day, for the kingdom that was stolen."

Thalia gave a half smile. "Sounds like a prince."

Brutus grinned. "Sounds like trouble."

Lyra did not speak, but the look she gave him was filled with quiet pride.

Above them, the stars broke through the treetops, cold and endless, like the road ahead. But beneath them, a fire burned.

And this time, it was not just for warmth.

The others slept, or pretended to.

Lyra sat apart from the camp, perched on a moss-covered rock beneath the outstretched limbs of a dead tree. Her bow rested across her lap, and a single arrow spun slowly between her fingers. Her hands always had to be doing something. She hated stillness. Stillness meant thinking.

Thinking meant remembering. And remembering hurt.

She glanced back at the flickering firelight. Kael sat on the other side, head dipped, talking softly with Thalia about patrol shifts. Brutus snored somewhere nearby, a rock of muscle and heart. Somehow, they made it feel like something close to safety.

She hated that too.

Because safety did not exist. Not really. Not for people like her.

She flicked the arrow upright, balancing it on one finger, then let it fall.

He's going to get himself killed.

The thought had echoed in her head ever since she met Kael. At first, it was simple. Obvious. A young man with fire in his chest and no idea how sharp the world's teeth really were. She had seen idealists before, naïve rebels who ended up in ditches with arrows in their backs.

But Kael was different.

He did not just fight with skill. He fought with purpose. With pain. And that look in his eyes, the one that saw you, not just your use.

She remembered the first time he stepped in front of her, blade drawn, back straight, when mercenaries tried to take her down in that canyon pass. No hesitation. No command. Just action.

No one had ever done that for her. Not since her brother.

Her fingers clenched the arrow until it splintered, a hairline crack down the shaft. She swore under her breath and tossed it aside.

You're a fool, Kael. And worse, you're making me believe in something again.

That was what terrified her most. Not the magic. Not Malrik. Not even the damned Wraithborn. But the idea that she might care too much. That she might stay.

And when Kael fell, as they all did eventually, what would be left of her?

A crunch of leaves made her head snap up. Kael stepped through the brush quietly, offering a small, tired smile.

"You always disappear after camp settles."

"I like the quiet," she said, more sharply than she meant.

He nodded, not pushing. "We will move at first light. Get some rest?"

She hesitated. Then, softer, "You're going to get yourself killed, you know."

Kael met her eyes, the fire reflected in his gaze. "Not today."

And somehow, she believed him.

He turned to go. Just before he stepped into the shadows, she called after him.

"Kael."

He paused.

She tossed him a fresh arrow from her quiver. "For when words aren't enough."

He caught it cleanly. “Thanks, Lyra.”

Then she whispered to the night, “Don’t make me lose someone else.”

The Whispering Ash – The Past of Lyra Ashveil

The first sound Lyra ever learned to recognize was the creak of the bowstring. Her family lived on the edges of Elaria, where forest and mountain met in untamed silence. Her brother, Darian, was her teacher, her shield, her hero. While their parents hunted and traded herbs to the border villages, Darian trained her relentlessly, turning childish games into drills until her hands bled from drawing the string.

But childhood was brief. A fever swept through the borderlands, cruel and quick. Within weeks, both her parents were gone, leaving her and Darian to fend for themselves. On her mother's final day, weak and fading, she pressed the family bow into Lyra's trembling hands. It was more than wood and string. It was a legacy, a burden, and a promise.

"Never let it fall silent," her mother whispered, breath barely clinging to her lips.

Those words seared themselves into Lyra's soul, an oath she carried from that moment on.

Darian had a dream for them both: to join the Wardens of Elaria, the elite scouts sworn to protect the realm's frontiers. Lyra was fire and impatience; Darian was steady and calm. Together, they balanced each other, two halves of a whole.

But dreams are fragile in a land already splintering under Malrik's shadow.

When Lyra was sixteen and Darian twenty, they were approached by Cairn, a Warden officer with a polished smile and honeyed words. He praised their skill, spoke of Elaria's need, and promised them a place if they proved themselves.

The mission he gave was simple: guide his men through the forest to ambush a band of mercenaries threatening the villages.

They believed him. They trusted him.

But Cairn was a viper in Warden's garb. The mercenaries were raiders sworn to Malrik, and the ambush was for Darian and Lyra themselves.

The night burned. Steel clashed in the dark as torches lit the trees with firelight. Darian fought like a lion, cutting down enemies with a fury Lyra had never seen before. She fired arrow after arrow until her fingers split, each shot a scream against betrayal. But numbers crushed them.

The image never leaves her: Darian's body shielding hers, Cairn's blade sliding into his back as he whispered hoarsely, "Run, Lyra." His blood covered her as he fell. She remembers the smirk on Cairn's face as he turned away, certain the raiders would finish her.

But Lyra ran. Not because she wanted to. Every instinct screamed to stay and die beside Darian, but his dying wish forced her to.

Lyra's world collapsed that night. She wandered, a half-dead girl with a bow and grief as her only companion. At first she sought vengeance, tracking raiders and striking them from the shadows with uncanny precision. But rage does not feed you. Revenge does not shelter you from storms.

Eventually, she became a sellsword, trading her bow to mercenary bands that valued skill more than loyalty. They called her strange, silent, always watching. She learned quickly: never trust too deeply, never linger too long. People died. Companions turned on each other for coin. She would not make the mistake again.

It was during these years she gained her name.

On one infamous night, a rival mercenary company betrayed her band for gold. Outnumbered and outflanked, her companions were slaughtered, and fires consumed the camp. Lyra alone survived, slipping through flame and shadow like a wraith, cutting down her hunters with arrows no one heard until it was too late. When dawn came, only ash and bodies remained.

Word spread: the girl who moves like smoke, who strikes without sound, leaving nothing but whispering ash behind.

And so she became Lyra of the Whispering Ash.

She wore the title like armor, burying the broken girl beneath it. Each job hardened her. Each betrayal carved another scar into her soul. She told herself feelings were a liability, loyalty a trap. The world was cruel; better to be the ghost in the fire than another corpse in it.

Years passed. Lyra thought she had become untouchable. But in truth, she was only drifting, a blade without purpose. Then fate brought her into the path of a young man named Kael.

When she first crossed him, she expected another naïve fool playing at hero. Yet Kael surprised her. He was not skilled, not yet, but he was unyielding. He carried pain in his eyes, the same hollow ache she knew. But unlike her, he bore it with hope. He had something she lost long ago: a dream bigger than vengeance.

At first she kept her distance. She mocked, she tested, she waited for him to break.

But Kael did not. He grew. And slowly, he began to remind her of Darian, not in face but in the unshakable belief that the fight was worth it, no matter the cost.

For the first time since the night of fire, Lyra felt something stir that she thought had died forever: the faint, dangerous spark of trust.

Lyra still carries Darian's broken dagger, its edge dulled, its hilt wrapped in bloodstained cloth. On nights when the fire burns low, she whispers to it, confessing her guilt, her rage, her fear of falling again. She has lived as shadow and ash, a ghost carved by betrayal.

But beside Kael, she begins to wonder if she can be something more. Not just the Whispering Ash.

But Lyra Ashveil, archer of Elaria.

And perhaps, one day, when Cairn's name surfaces again, she will have the chance to finish the vow she made over her brother's body: to strike down betrayal itself with an arrow loosed from the ashes of the past.

Chapter 13 - The Road to Emberdeep

The morning after the Wraithborn battle dawned cold and damp. Fog clung to the forest like a second skin, curling between branches and around the group as they broke camp in silence. No one spoke much, not even Brutus, who usually had a joke to break the tension.

Kael felt the weight of it all. Of leadership. Of survival. Of what he now carried.

They had faced something ancient, something born of Malrik's dark legacy, and survived. But only just. Thalia's magic was still unstable, and Lyra's shoulder wound had worsened despite her defiance. Brutus had a gash down his ribs that he refused to let anyone inspect. Kael himself had not slept. The Wraithborn's eyes haunted him. Hollow. Endless.

Like Malrik had been watching.

As they walked, Kael hung back from the group, eyes scanning the path ahead. They were heading southeast now, toward Emberdeep, a trading city near the border of the old kingdom's heartlands. Thorne had told him there might be a safehouse there. And answers.

Lyra caught up beside him, walking with practiced silence. "Still brooding, Your Highness?"

He gave a tired smile. "Thinking."

She nudged him with her elbow. "Try not to do too much of that. Might sprain something."

He chuckled. "Thanks for the concern."

“I charge extra for emotional support.”

Behind them, Thalia was quietly muttering to herself, violet eyes flickering with unstable aether. Kael had noticed her spacing out more often. He knew it was not just the magic. It was fear. Of what she could become. Of what she already was.

Brutus lumbered beside her, keeping a watchful eye. He had taken to guarding her like an older brother. Kael had said nothing, but it warmed him to see it.

After a moment of hesitation, Kael slowed his pace and fell in beside Thalia. “How’s the staff?” he asked quietly.

Her fingers tightened around the obsidian shaft, the violet gem pulsing faintly with her heartbeat. “It helps,” she admitted, voice low.

“It channels the chaos, keeps it from tearing me apart. But...” Her lips pressed together, eyes glimmering with something heavier than exhaustion. “It can’t change what I am.”

Kael studied her. “And what’s that?”

Her gaze flicked toward him, sharp but vulnerable. “Half demon. Half human. My magic was never meant to be stable. The blood inside me fights itself every day. That’s why I lose control.”

Kael said nothing, letting her speak.

“My family knew what I was. They tried to teach me to control it, to bind the chaos with discipline. We were guardians once, protectors of the Dragonfire Crown. For generations, we stood watch over it, ensuring its power was never misused.” Her voice wavered, then steadied with a kind of haunted pride. “But Malrik feared us. He sent his generals to hunt us down. I was just a child when they came. I remember fire. Screams. My father's last words were to run. So I did."

Kael frowned. "The Dragonfire Crown... what is it, really?"

Thalia shook her head, her violet eyes dimming. "I don't know. Only that it was older than kingdoms. My family never spoke its secrets, not even to me. We were taught only that it was dangerous, sacred, and that we must guard it with our lives."

Her fingers brushed the glowing gem of the staff, her expression distant. "And that was enough for Malrik to hate us. Enough to kill us all."

She fell silent for a moment before adding, almost in a whisper, "When I saw the shard of the Crown in Var'Lath, it was like it called to me. Maybe because of my blood. Or maybe because I was meant to find you, Kael."

The prince's chest tightened, her words weighing on him like another stone added to an already heavy load. They were not just following him because of his birthright. Each of them carried scars, legacies, and broken pieces of Malrik's cruelty. And they were all looking to him to forge something out of the wreckage.

Kael forced his voice steady. "Then you're not running anymore. None of us are. Malrik took enough from us. We fight back, together."

Thalia's lips curved in the faintest, almost reluctant smile. "Together, then."

She gripped the staff tighter, and for the first time since the ruins, her eyes held more than fear. They held resolve.

Kael turned back to the road ahead. The weight of leadership pressed harder against his shoulders, but so did the certainty that they were not just following him. They were entrusting him with everything they had left.

And that made failure unthinkable.

They made camp that night near a crumbling watchtower, a relic of the old kingdom. While the others gathered firewood and checked rations, Kael climbed the narrow, broken stairs to the top.

The wind hit him like a slap, cold and sharp.

From the height, the forest stretched endlessly in every direction. Beautiful. Unforgiving.

He thought of what lay ahead. Malrik would know by now. About the Wraithborn. About them.

This was not just a journey anymore. It was a rebellion in its first breath. Still fragile. Still unformed.

But breathing.

Footsteps echoed behind him. Thalia.

"You shouldn't be alone," she said, hugging her arms tightly. "Your aura is unsettled."

Kael raised a brow. "Is that a magical diagnosis?"

"It's a feeling. Which, apparently, I'm allowed to have now."

He turned, leaning back against the stone. "I'm trying to figure out who I need to be."

"Try being yourself, maybe?"

He laughed bitterly. “That’s the one person I don’t know how to be anymore.”

She stepped beside him, looking out at the moonlit forest. “Then build him from the pieces that survived.”

For a moment, neither of them spoke.

Then Thalia said softly, “You inspire people, Kael. Not because you’re perfect. But because you fight like you’re already broken, and still keep going.”

Kael looked at her. “Do you believe in me, Thalia?”

She smiled faintly. “I’m still deciding. But I'm here.”

That was enough.

He looked back out into the dark, the wind tearing at his cloak. Malrik ruled from the shadows. But Kael was no longer running.

Interlude - The Winds Change

The Whispering Wilds were quiet that night. Too quiet.

General Thorne stood on a crag overlooking the ravine below, the wind tugging at the edges of his cloak. Moonlight silvered his scarred face, casting deep shadows beneath his eyes. His hand rested on the hilt of the great sword at his back, not out of habit but out of something older. An ache he could not name.

He had felt it an hour ago, a pulse beneath his ribs. Faint, but undeniable. Not danger. Not death.

Change.

He exhaled slowly, eyes scanning the stars beyond the tree line. He remembered the boy who once tripped over his own feet trying to swing a wooden sword. The boy who refused to cry even when his hands bled. The boy who stood in front of a charging Direfang to protect a wounded sparrow.

That boy was still out there.

But now he walked beside strangers. Faced monsters older than empires. And carried a burden heavier than blood.

Thorne reached into his coat and withdrew an old piece of parchment. The edges were worn and the ink had faded, but he knew the words by heart.

"When fire rises from the fallen crown, the storm shall follow. And the heir must choose vengeance... or victory."

He folded it again and slipped it away.

Kael had begun the path. The heir was no longer running.

Thorne closed his eyes. "The boy becomes a leader," he murmured, voice low. "But God help him if he forgets to be a son."

The wind shifted then, soft but certain, carrying the scent of ash and iron.

Thorne turned back toward the small camp behind him, where the scouts still slept, unaware.

He would not interfere yet.

But the time was coming when the shadows would reach deeper. When Kael would face not just Malrik, but the ghosts that waited in his own heart.

Thorne's grip tightened. And when that moment came, he would be ready.

Interlude - The Ashen Table

A storm raged over Castle Noctis, but the lightning dared not strike the spires. It veered away, as if the very sky feared the man seated beneath its shadow.

Lord Malrik leaned over the Ashen Table, a cursed slab of obsidian used only during wartime. Its surface shifted like dark water, forming images from across the realm: Kael's face, Lyra's bow drawn, Brutus in battle stance, Thalia ablaze with unstable magic. Each image dissolved under his hand, smearing into black streaks.

"They're headed to Emberdeep," Malrik muttered, voice like a whetstone scraping steel. "That grave of rebellion is still breathing after all these years."

He slammed his fist down. The table cracked.

A moment later, the war room doors opened, not with ceremony but with menace.

The Four War Generals of the Crimson Veil stepped into the torch-lit gloom, each a monster shaped by war and sorcery.

First came General Veska, blade mistress of the Umbra Legions. She did not walk; she glided forward on a thick fog of smoke that followed her like chained spirits. Her armor was crimson and black, every inch shaped like the edge of a dagger. Her bone-and-shadowsteel mask covered her face completely, save for two slits that glowed faint red. She knelt in silence, smoke spilling around her.

"Veska," Malrik said, his voice cold. "Your spies failed me."

"No, my king," Veska whispered. "They were never meant to return. Their deaths bought us knowledge."

"Not enough," Malrik snapped. "Knowledge does not bleed."

A gust of heated wind announced General Virex, the Flame of the Witherlands. Her deep crimson armor pulsed with heat, veins of fire alive beneath its surface. She drew her sword slowly, and as it left the sheath it ignited, casting fiery light across the chamber. Her lips curled into a smile as sparks kissed the stone floor.

"Let me raze Emberdeep. There will be no refuge, only fire."

"You burned the Witherlands to cinders," Malrik said flatly. "Do not think I forgot the screams."

"You enjoyed them," Virex replied, without shame.

A hollow silence crept in before General Sevrak, the Pale Flame, entered. His pale robes barely touched the ground. Fire swirled faintly around his hands, but it gave no light, no warmth. It simply was. His expression was unreadable, and his voice chilled the marrow.

"They carry the Phoenix sigil. The old magic may awaken if Kael enters the ruins beneath Emberdeep."

"Then erase it," Malrik growled.

"Erasure is not simple," Sevrak replied. "But I will try." The chamber darkened further.

General Mercurius, the half-blood demon, arrived last, stepping from a swirl of shadows. His dark-blue armor shimmered like oil over water, and his shadow blade curled unnaturally in his hand. Crimson eyes locked with Malrik's, and for a moment the air itself seemed to shrink.

“Let them hope,” Mercurius said smoothly. “Let them think they’ve found strength. And when they begin to believe, break them.”

Malrik paced slowly around the Ashen Table, considering his generals with eyes like black flame.

“You speak of hope and ruins like toys on a shelf. But this boy, Kael, he’s beginning to become something dangerous.”

He paused, then clenched his hand. The flickering image of Kael on the table shattered into smoke.

“He leads now, not just fights. And fools are starting to follow.” His voice dipped, full of venom. “So burn his symbols. Corrupt his legends. Turn his allies, one by one, until even the light fears him.”

He looked to all four generals. “Divide. Hunt. Bleed them. Emberdeep must fall before it rises.”

As the storm outside Castle Noctis screamed louder, the four war generals bowed in unison and vanished like nightmares at sunrise. Malrik sat alone once more, staring at the cracked Ashen Table.

“Let them think they walk toward salvation,” he whispered. “They walk into the mouth of a dragon.”

Chapter 14 - Return to Emberdeep

The mountain air of Emberdeep carried the scent of coal smoke and cold iron. Jagged peaks loomed in the distance, their snow-capped crowns glimmering faintly beneath a sky awash in amber light. The fortified city lay cradled between two cliffs, its high blackstone walls bristling with spearpoints and watchtowers.

Kael walked at the head of the group, his boots crunching over the frost-hardened earth. Lyra kept pace beside him, the faint smile on her lips betraying her relief at seeing the familiar skyline. Brutus ambled behind them, massive arms crossed, while Thalia kept a wary eye on the guards posted along the wall, her violet gaze never still.

At the gates, a familiar figure stepped forward. Broad-shouldered, clad in dark steel plate etched with the crest of the Fallen Crown, General Thorne stood like an unmovable wall. His weathered face softened slightly when his eyes landed on Kael, though the flicker of relief was quickly masked by discipline.

“You have grown,” Thorne said.

“And you have been busy,” Kael replied.

The two clasped forearms, the contact firm and weighted with unspoken history.

Thorne’s gaze shifted past Kael, taking in Brutus first. The hulking warrior tilted his head in greeting, his tusked grin widening.

“So this is the one who broke the Colosseum’s champion? I expected taller,” Thorne said.

Brutus snorted. "And I expected older. Guess we are both disappointed."

Before the banter could escalate, Thorne's attention moved to Thalia. She met his eyes without a shred of deference, her presence sharp as the edge of a dagger.

"Mage," Thorne said.

"General," she replied.

No warmth. Only the cold acknowledgment of two predators sizing each other up.

Finally, Thorne turned to Lyra. His voice lowered so only she could hear.

"How has he been?"

Her gaze flicked to Kael, who was busy answering Brutus's booming question about Emberdeep's forges. Lyra's smile was faint but genuine.

"He is learning. He stumbles sometimes, but he does not let us fall. He is not just fighting beside us. He is making us want to follow," she said.

Thorne did not respond right away. His eyes lingered on Kael, reading every shift in the young man's posture, every choice in how he moved. Finally, a quiet hum of approval escaped him.

"Good. He will need that for what is coming."

The gates of Emberdeep groaned open, and the group stepped inside. The clang of hammers and roar of forges filled the air, the city alive with the pulse of industry. But beneath it all, there was tension in the streets. Eyes watched from shadowed alleys, and whispers darted like rats through the crowd.

Kael could feel it too. Emberdeep was strong, but it was bracing for something.

They walked through the main corridor toward the inner fortress, passing smiths, soldiers, and tired workers. As they entered the great hall, Thorne's expression hardened.

"If we are going to strike against Malrik's empire, you need to know what you are walking into. He does not just sit on that throne. He has wrapped himself in monsters. The Four Generals of the Crimson Veil."

The air in the hall seemed to tighten with the weight of those words.

Thorne turned, pacing slowly before them as if summoning their faces from memory.

"First, General Veska. Blade Mistress of the Umbra Legions. She moves across the battlefield like smoke. Her robes are a living shadow, and her face is hidden behind a mask of bone and shadowsteel. Crimson and black are her colors. She commands assassins, saboteurs, and the kind of war that does not announce itself."

Lyra's jaw clenched. Thalia's fingers brushed the edge of her spell focus as if already imagining how she would counter someone like that.

"Second, General Virex, the Flame of the Witherlands. Once, her name was Vie. She was Elarian before the fire claimed her. She wears armor forged in the heart of a burning land. When she draws her sword, it ignites. They say entire battalions have turned to ash beneath her flames."

Kael's hand instinctively went to the hilt of his sword. He did not know why, but the name struck something deep in his chest, like distant thunder.

“Third, General Sevrak, the Pale Flame. A pyromancer unlike any other. His fire does not burn. It erases. Stone, flesh, steel. It leaves nothing but silence behind. No smoke. No screams. Just gone.”

A chill passed through the group, colder than Emberdeep wind.

“And last, General Mercurius. A half-blood demon who wields dark magic like a blade. His armor is deep blue, his power older than Malrik's reign. Some call him the Warlock of the Hollow Vale. Wherever he walks, shadows follow.”

Thorne finally faced Kael.

“These are not mere soldiers. Each commands legions and can turn the tide of war alone. You will meet them soon enough. But you had better be ready when you do.”

Silence settled over the hall. The weight of Thorne’s words pressed against their shoulders, not to crush them but to temper them.

Kael nodded once, steady, his eyes hardening with quiet fire.

“Then we will be ready.”

Outside, the forges roared. Inside, the war began to take shape.

Chapter 15 – Ashes Beneath Emberdeep

The cavernous hall of Emberdeep's inner keep was alive with the sound of the forges.
The clang of hammer upon steel carried faintly through stone passages, each strike ringing like a heartbeat deep within the mountain's bones. Lanternlight trembled along blackened walls, their soot-dark faces etched with scars of fire and smoke. Emberdeep had been born from the mountain's flame and nearly perished in it; the air was heavy with the scent of charred stone and iron, a reminder that this fortress had endured both the choking heat of war and the cold silence that followed defeat.

Kael sat at the war table, his hand tracing the rough etchings carved into its surface. The table itself was no polished relic. It was scarred, chipped, gouged from years of desperate planning. A map had been spread across its breadth, parchment stained with soot and sweat. Red markings wound their way across it like veins of blood, showing the path of Malrik's relentless advances. Each line pressed deeper into lands that had once belonged to Elaria, villages devoured like morsels, strongholds reduced to rubble.

His finger lingered on one such mark: Ashmore Downs. Once a quiet place of shepherds and barley fields, now nothing but blackened ruins. Kael's jaw tightened.

Across from him, Thalia leaned on her staff, her violet eyes glowing faintly in the lanternlight. She looked as weary as he felt, her posture betraying the fatigue of constant vigilance. Yet even in her fatigue, there was focus. Her voice, when she finally spoke, was soft but certain.

"You trace those lines as if they might change beneath your touch. They won't. Not until Malrik himself is stopped."

Kael didn't look up. "I know. But every line is a village lost. Every mark is a failure I carry."

Thalia tilted her head, her long hair falling across one shoulder like ink spilling across parchment. "It isn't failure, Kael. It is inheritance. You carry the weight of what Malrik has done because it is your burden to undo."

Near the wall, Lyra stood with her back pressed to the cold stone. Her arms were crossed, her bow leaning against her shoulder, and her sharp green eyes never stopped moving. She had taken the role of watchman even here, as though Kael required protection from the shadows themselves. Her silence was not disinterest but vigilance. She guarded Kael not only from threats of steel but from the quiet, corrosive doubts that could gnaw at him when the weight grew too heavy.

Brutus, however, could not keep still. The orc paced the hall like a wolf forced into too small a cage, tusks bared in a restless scowl. His heavy boots thudded against the stone, each step echoing frustration.

"I don't like it," Brutus rumbled, finally breaking the silence. "Ruins are one thing, but Emberdeep's tunnels? That's a deathtrap waiting to happen."

Kael raised his eyes at last, meeting the orc's with calm determination. "Which is exactly why Malrik won't expect us to move through them."

Brutus snorted, tusks gleaming as he bared them in half a sneer. "Or maybe he will expect it because only madmen would try."

A low rumble of boots drew all eyes to the doorway. Thorne entered, his armor catching the dim light like muted fire. Time had etched deep lines into his weathered face, his hair even more gray now than black, but his gaze was sharp, his posture unyielding. His presence carried the quiet weight of authority, forged not from rank alone but from the scars of battle and years of survival.

He approached the war table with slow, deliberate steps, his eyes scanning the map with a soldier's measured care. When he finally spoke, his voice was gravel: low, steady, commanding.

“You have chosen the southern passage?”

Kael straightened. “It gives us the best chance to reach the Witherlands without drawing attention.”

Thorne's hand brushed along the map, tracing the jagged edge of the mountains. His expression did not soften. "The southern passage will take you beneath the Blackspire range. If Veska's Umbra Legions are stationed anywhere nearby, you will be walking straight into the jaws of the beast.”

Kael did not flinch. “Then we will be ready.”

The words hung in the air, heavy and dangerous. Brutus gave a low growl, Thalia's violet eyes narrowed, and Lyra's green gaze flicked to Kael with a mixture of pride and worry.

Thorne studied the young man for a long moment, as if weighing his soul against the steel of his resolve. At last, he gave a small, solemn nod.

“We move at first light.”

That night, Emberdeep was quieter. The roar of the forges had dulled to a low hum, and the great halls lay cloaked in the dim orange glow of dying embers. Soldiers and smiths slept where they could: some on cots, others slumped against anvils, their exhaustion greater than any need for comfort. Refugees huddled in the corners of the keep, their eyes hollow, their children clutching scraps of bread as if they were treasure.

Kael found himself drawn to the high balcony overlooking the valley beyond. The air was cool here, touched with the faint scent of pine carried down from the mountains. Below, the valley lay in shadow, a sea of black trees swaying under the moonlight.

To Kael, it looked less like a forest and more like a tide of darkness waiting to surge over them all.

He gripped the balcony's stone railing, staring out into the night. The closer they came to Malrik, the heavier the weight pressed upon him. It was not fear of death; he had long made peace with that. It was the crushing awareness that every step drew him nearer to a reckoning he could not afford to lose.

“You have been carrying more lately.”

Lyra’s voice was soft, almost hesitant. He turned to her standing a few paces behind, her silver-blonde hair catching the moonlight. She had shed her armor, wearing only a simple tunic, though her bow was never far from reach.

Kael exhaled slowly. “The closer we get to Malrik, the heavier it feels.”

Lyra’s expression softened. She stepped closer, her voice gentle but firm. “That is what leadership is, Kael. You bear it so the rest of us don't have to.”

Her words lingered between them like an unspoken oath, binding and fragile. For a moment, Kael felt something ease within him. Not the weight lifted, but steadied, as if her presence had given him a second hand upon the burden. He managed a faint smile.

“Then I’ll carry it for as long as I must.”

Lyra's gaze lingered on him, unreadable. She wanted to say more. He could see it in the parting of her lips, the tension in her stance. But instead she turned and left him to the night.

The next morning, Emberdeep stirred before the sun rose. Its people lived by firelight and the rhythm of hammer strikes, so dawn was measured not in sunlight but in the renewal of labor.

The training grounds were a cavern hollowed from the mountainside, lit by hanging braziers and the glow of molten slag trickling from the forges above. Kael walked among the soldiers there: some seasoned, scarred veterans, others little more than boys gripping blades too large for their hands. Their armor was mismatched, a patchwork of salvaged iron and dwarven steel, but their eyes carried a fierce, hungry light.

Brutus joined them, his heavy tread echoing like drumbeats. The orc folded his arms as he watched a pair of young recruits sparring with wooden staves. Their movements were clumsy, strikes too slow, footwork unsure. Brutus let out a snort that startled both of them into dropping their weapons.

"You fight like chickens pecking grain," he said, stepping into the circle. He shoved one recruit aside and snatched a staff from the other, twirling it with deceptive grace for someone of his bulk. "Watch."

He struck with the speed of a striking serpent, the staff cracking against the boy's wrist before he could blink. The boy yelped, clutching his arm, but Brutus only grinned, baring tusks.

"You will heal. Pain is a better teacher than mercy." He looked around at the circle of wide eyes. "Out there, mercy will get you killed."

Kael caught the orc's gaze and gave a small nod. Brutus was harsh, but he was right. These people could not afford softness anymore.

Thalia, meanwhile, had gathered a cluster of wounded in another corner. Her staff glowed faintly as she traced runes of healing across bandaged flesh. She moved with quiet patience, her voice a soothing murmur as she coaxed the flow of arcane energy into cuts and burns. For every wound she closed, another soldier found the strength to stand straighter.

Lyra remained in the shadows, as always. She perched on a ledge above the training ground, bow across her lap, watching with hawk-like vigilance. At first Kael thought she was keeping lookout, but then he noticed the way her eyes followed his every step. She was guarding him, as though even here, surrounded by allies, danger could come crawling from the dark. Perhaps it could.

When Kael reached her perch, she did not look up.
“You’re walking the grounds like you already wear the crown," she said softly.

“I don’t,” Kael replied.

“You will,” she countered, green eyes glinting. “Whether you want to or not.”
Kael had no answer.

Kael lingered in the training cavern after the others had left, staring at the abandoned practice dummies. Straw spilled from their slashed bellies like entrails, and the floor was littered with splinters. He was about to turn away when he felt a tug at his cloak.

He looked down.

A boy no older than eight stood there, thin as a reed, his tunic patched so many times it was more stitch than fabric. His eyes were wide, brown as river mud, and in his hands he clutched a wooden toy sword, little more than a stick shaved into shape.

"You're him," the boy whispered.

Kael crouched so they were eye to eye.
"Who am I?" he asked gently.

The boy hesitated, chewing his lip.
"The one who fights Malrik. The one they say won't stop."

Kael felt something twist in his chest. He wanted to deny it, to tell the child not to place faith where it could be broken. But he could not.

Instead, he asked, "What's your name?"

"Ronan."

"Ronan," Kael repeated softly. "Did you lose someone?"

The boy's eyes dropped to the toy sword.
"My father. In Ash Vale. He told me to keep this. Said I'd need it to protect Mother and my sister."

Kael swallowed, fighting the ache in his throat. He reached out and touched the boy's shoulder.
"Your father was brave."

Ronan looked up, tears brimming but unshed.
"Will you make him pay? Will you make Malrik pay?"

Kael should have answered with fire, with the steel of vengeance. But as he stared into those fragile, desperate eyes, he felt the weight of something greater.

"I'll fight," Kael said at last. "Not just to make Malrik pay, but so your sister grows up in a world where she doesn't need that sword."

Ronan blinked at him, then did something unexpected. He wrapped his thin arms around Kael's neck and hugged him.

It lasted only a moment before the boy darted away into the shadows of the cavern. But Kael stayed kneeling, frozen, the warmth of that brief embrace burning deeper than any wound.

For the first time that night, he understood what Thorne had meant. Leadership was not about crowns or thrones or commands shouted over battlefields. It was about the small hands that reached for you in the dark, believing you would not let go.

Later, in the mess hall, the companions gathered. Emberdeep's kitchens were humble, with stone hearths, iron cauldrons, and dwarven-built spits turning slowly above low fires. Soldiers lined up for bowls of stew made from root vegetables and salted meat, food thick and heavy enough to sustain another day's labor.

Brutus ate like a man starved, tearing bread in half with tusks bared, while Lyra picked carefully at hers. Thalia ate with slow precision, her fingers never hurried. Kael ate little at all, though he forced himself to chew for strength's sake.

Thorne entered near the end of the meal. His presence silenced the room as naturally as a storm hushes the wind. Soldiers straightened, whispers stilled, and all eyes turned toward him. Yet he ignored them, striding directly to Kael's table.

He sat without ceremony, setting aside his gauntlets with a metallic clink. His gray eye fixed on Kael with the weight of unspoken truths.

"You lead them well enough," Thorne said at last, his voice rough as gravel. "But don't mistake obedience for faith. They will follow you into the tunnels tomorrow because I tell them to. What happens after, that is on you."

Kael straightened. "I'll earn their faith."

Thorne's gaze sharpened, measuring him.
"And how will you do that? By promising vengeance? By waving a blade forged in your father's name? The crown does not earn loyalty, boy. Blood does. Sweat does. Standing in front of them when death comes does."

The words cut deep, but Kael forced himself to meet them with steady eyes.
"Then I'll bleed first."

A silence stretched between them. Then, for the first time in days, Thorne's mouth twitched, almost but not quite a smile.

"You remind me of your father when you speak like that," he said quietly. "And your mother when you don't let me see fear in your eyes."

The words struck Kael harder than any blade. He had grown used to Thorne's stoicism and his lessons of steel and discipline, but rarely did the man allow sentiment to bleed through. It was like a crack in a fortress wall, a glimpse of the man beneath the armor.

Before Kael could respond, Thorne rose.
"We leave at first light. Until then, rest. You will need every breath of strength."

He walked away, boots echoing across stone, and Kael was left with the echo of his parents' memory burning in his chest.

That night, Emberdeep seemed to breathe. Fire burned low, casting long shadows across the halls. Refugees whispered prayers in the corners, children clutching their mothers. Soldiers polished weapons, checked armor straps, and tried to sleep on cold stone floors.

Kael could not sleep. He found himself once more on the balcony, staring at the dark valley.

Brutus joined him this time, carrying a skin of ale. The orc leaned heavily against the stone rail, swigged deep, then passed it to Kael.

"You look like a man about to be crushed under his own armor," Brutus said.

Kael took a drink. The ale was bitter, strong enough to burn. "Maybe I am."

Brutus grinned.
"Good. Means you're thinking. A leader who doesn't think is a corpse waiting for dirt."

It was crude wisdom, but it lightened Kael's chest. He almost laughed.

Far across the mountains, in Malrik's throne hall, the council of war gathered.

Virex slammed her blade into the stone floor, sparks leaping. "Give me the word, and I will march my legion through the Black Spires. Emberdeep will drown in flame before the week is out."

Malrik did not answer. He reclined in his throne of shadowsteel, black fire coiling around him like smoke. His gaze swept across his generals, weighing each with the patience of a predator.

"No," he said at last. His voice was low, but it carried like thunder. "Let them believe they are safe in their mountain tomb. Let them walk the tunnels and chokc on thcir hopc."

He turned his gaze to Veska, who knelt unmoving.
"Your Umbra Legions will be the jaws in the dark. Cut them off. Cripple them. Leave enough survivors to crawl back to Emberdeep with stories of despair."

Veska inclined her head, her bone and shadowsteel mask gleaming.
"As you command."

Sevrak stepped forward, his hollow eyes glinting in the gloom. His voice was soft, almost reverent.
"What would you have of me, my lord?"

Malrik's gaze lingered on him a moment before shifting to the map etched across the obsidian floor.
"Not yet. Your time will come. I will tell you when and where to strike. For now, watch. Wait. Let the boy believe he still has a path forward."

Mercurius chuckled, leaning lazily against his blade.
"You play with him like a wolf toys with a rabbit. But even rabbits bite when cornered."

Malrik's gaze flickered to him, sharp as a knife.
"And when they do, we break their teeth."

The generals bowed again, the air thick with promise.

Back in Emberdeep, Kael returned to his quarters. Lyra was waiting there, perched on the edge of a chair with her bow across her knees. She did not speak at first, only studied him with those sharp eyes that saw more than he wanted her to.

"You're ready," she said finally.

Kael shook his head.
"No one's ever ready for this."

"Then you're as ready as anyone can be."

Her words were not meant to comfort, but they did. Kael sat across from her, the silence between them heavy and unspoken. For a moment, he allowed himself to breathe, to simply exist without the weight of destiny pressing down on his shoulders.

Tomorrow, the tunnels awaited. And beyond them, war.

Interlude - The Weight of the Coming Storm

The fires of Emberdeep's forge district had burned low, their glow fading to dull embers beneath the night sky. The mountain winds whispered against the fortress walls, carrying with them the scent of snow from the high peaks.

General Thorne stood alone on a balcony overlooking the sleeping city, his gauntleted hands resting on the cold stone railing. The muffled clamor of the day had long since died, replaced by the faint creak of banners shifting in the breeze.

Below, Kael's quarters were lit by a single candle. Thorne could just make out the prince's silhouette moving inside, sorting gear, tending to his sword, pacing. Always pacing.

Thorne's jaw tightened.
He's stronger. Sharper. But strength alone will not carry him through what is coming.

His mind drifted to Malrik's name, a shadow stretching far beyond the horizon. And now, word had reached Emberdeep of Malrik's gathering war council, four generals, each one a nightmare in their own right. Thorne had faced armies before, but this would be different.

He thought of the faces he had met that day. Brutus, brutal but loyal. Thalia, cold, calculating, and likely dangerous in her own way. Lyra, devoted to Kael, though there was something in her eyes, a storm she had not named.

He's found people worth bleeding for, Thorne mused. But will they be enough to keep him alive, or will they be the weight that drags him under?

The candle in Kael's window flickered, then went out. Darkness claimed the room. Thorne lingered a moment longer, his hand tightening into a fist.

As he turned and walked back into the shadows of the fortress, his voice carried on the cold wind following him like a silent omen. "You've got fire boy. But fire burns out fast." Looking back into the darkness, "and Malrik will do anything to try and snuff it out."

Chapter 16 - Shadows in the Deep

The night they descended into Emberdeep's southern tunnels, the fortress was alive with quiet dread. Men and women of the rebellion gathered in the old halls, their weapons spread out on rough-hewn tables, their armor patched with mismatched scraps of steel and leather. The forges roared deep in the belly of the keep, the pounding of hammers echoing like a heartbeat beneath the stone.

Kael stood at the edge of it all, watching. He had learned long ago to hide the weight pressing on him, but tonight it was heavier than usual. Every decision he made led lives into danger. Every order risked the fragile hope they had built from the ashes of Elaria's fall.

Brutus was sharpening his axe at one of the side tables, grinding the whetstone with enough force to shower sparks. The orc's usual grin was gone, his jaw clenched, his shoulders set like stone. Lyra inspected her bowstring, running her fingers along the wood with the precision of ritual. Thalia sat quietly, eyes closed, lips moving in silent incantation, her spells etched in memory long before they would be needed.

The hall smelled of oil, sweat, and steel. And beneath it all, the faint scent of fear.

Thorne emerged from the shadows near the war table. His armor was strapped, sword at his side, his cloak black as the stone itself. He studied Kael for a moment before speaking.

"You have chosen your path," Thorne said. His voice carried the weight of someone who had walked this road many times before. "But remember, paths through the dark are never straight. Doubt will come. Fear will whisper. Your soldiers will look to you to silence both."

Kael met his gaze. “And if I falter?”

Thorne’s mouth curved into something that was almost a smile. “Then they will fall with you. So do not falter.”

It was harsh, but Kael knew it was meant as trust. Thorne did not waste words on those he thought incapable.

Around them, more rebels prepared. Kael counted twenty-four in all, though only a handful had seen real battle. Some were farmers turned fighters, others smiths who had traded hammers for swords. Among them was a lean man with a scar tracing his jawline. Kirros. He moved with an ease that marked him as more seasoned than the rest, his eyes sharp, his words quiet. He carried himself like someone used to survival, and the soldiers gave him respect.

Kael had taken note of him before, but tonight he found himself watching longer. Kirros’s loyalty had not yet been proven. Still, in war, beggars could not be choosers.

A tug at his cloak drew Kael’s attention downward. A boy, perhaps no more than nine, stood before him. His clothes were ragged, too large for his thin frame, and his eyes were wide with awe. In his small hands he clutched a wooden carving of a bird, wings outstretched as if frozen mid-flight.

“My father carved it,” the boy whispered. “He said you were the one who could make the skies safe again. I want you to have it.”

Kael crouched, taking the carving with care. The wood was rough, but it bore the marks of patient craftsmanship. He closed his hand around it, feeling its weight.

“Thank you,” Kael said softly. “I will carry it with me. And I will do everything I can to make sure the skies belong to you again.”

The boy nodded, eyes shining, then ran back to the cluster of refugees at the far wall.

The carving stayed in Kael's pocket as they gathered at the tunnel mouth. The entrance yawned before them, a jagged crack in the southern face of Emberdeep, guarded by the shadows of the mountain. Torches flared, casting orange light on damp stone. The air that seeped from within was cold, as if the mountain itself exhaled frost.

Kael looked back at his company. Two dozen rebels stood ready, their faces lit by firelight. Some clutched weapons too large for them, others carried shields dented from years of disuse. Yet every one of them stood tall.

Thorne's voice broke the silence. "Beyond these stones is no glory, no song. Only shadow and the waiting teeth of Malrik's hounds. Hold the line, hold each other, and you may yet see dawn."

The rebels murmured assent.

Brutus hefted his axe. "Then what are we waiting for? Let's get moving before the mountain swallows its courage."

The first breath inside the tunnels was colder than Kael expected, an icy exhale from the mountain's depths. Their torches hissed and sputtered, flames struggling against the damp. The walls were slick with condensation, glistening like veins of black glass. Each step echoed, swallowed quickly by the stone.

Brutus led, his bulk a shield in the dark. Kael followed, hand on the hilt of his sword. Lyra kept her bow drawn, eyes scanning the shadows. Thalia whispered enchantments to keep the torches alive, her voice a constant rhythm in the silence. Thorne walked just behind Kael, silent but present.

The deeper they went, the quieter the world became, until only the sound of dripping water remained. The rebels moved in tight formation, nerves taut. Kael glanced back now and then, catching fragments of whispered prayers, clenched jaws, white knuckles gripping spears.

A faint metallic scrape echoed ahead. Kael raised his hand, halting the column. Brutus stilled, nostrils flaring.

“We are not alone,” Brutus growled.

“Footsteps,” Lyra whispered. “Too light to be miners.”

A swirl of smoke slithered across the tunnel floor, vanishing into a side passage.

They pressed forward cautiously. Soon the tunnel opened into a collapsed hall, where shattered columns lay like bones. Carvings marked the walls, jagged sigils curling like thorns.

“Umbra markings,” Thalia whispered. Her violet eyes glowed faintly in the torchlight. “Veska’s hand. We should turn back.”

“No,” Kael said firmly. “If they are here, I need to know how close.”

A sudden rush of air extinguished their torches. Darkness fell like a blade.

Shapes descended from above, shadows clinging to walls, eyes glinting through black veils. Chains and steel whispered as Umbra scouts emerged, their movements unnaturally fluid.

Lyra lit an arrow and fired into the dark. For a moment, the fire revealed them, bone and shadowsteel masks grinning like skulls, blades curved and dripping with black resin.

The clash was immediate. Brutus roared, cleaving one scout in half. Kael's sword flashed, cutting through another's ribs. The rebels surged, their cries of defiance echoing against stone.

But the Umbra Legion was faster, sharper. They struck with precision, each blade finding gaps in armor. A rebel fell to Kael's right, his throat opened. Another screamed as chains wrapped around his legs, dragging him into shadow.

Kael fought like a storm, but with every scout slain, two more seemed to appear. Ink-dark residue slicked the ground where their bodies dissolved, clinging like tar.

"They were not here to fight," Brutus snarled, pulling his axe free from one. "They were marking us."

Kael's heart sank. Veska knew.

Then the shadows deepened, and she came.

Veska stepped from the darkness as if it parted for her, her bone and shadowsteel mask gleaming in the dim light. Her blades, curved and hungry, dripped black smoke. She moved like water, like death given form.

The rebels faltered at the sight of her. Kael felt their fear, heavy as stone. He forced himself forward.

"Hold the line!" he shouted, his voice ringing against the cavern walls. "She bleeds like the rest of them!"

But did she?

Veska struck, and the rebellion bled.

Kael's world became a blur of screams, steel, and shadow. He saw rebels he had spoken to only hours before, men who had shared their names, women who had spoken of children left behind, cut down before his eyes. Their deaths carved themselves into him, one after another, but he could not falter. Because if he did, all of them would die.

The last of the Umbra scouts dissolved into black vapor, leaving the cavern quiet again, though the silence was worse than the clash of steel. The rebels stood in a ragged circle, panting, weapons slick with dark residue that clung to steel and skin alike. Torches sputtered weakly, casting jagged shadows across the ruined hall.

Then the shadows shifted.

From the far side of the cavern, a figure emerged, tall and lean, armored in bone and shadowsteel. Veska. She did not rush them, nor lift her blade. She only stood, her mask tilted as if studying prey already snared.

A few rebels raised their weapons, but Kael lifted his hand, halting them. The air was too still, too heavy. Veska's presence alone seemed to choke the hall.

Her gaze, though hidden, lingered on Kael. For a moment, he felt her eyes strip away his armor. She stepped backward into the dark. Shadows swallowed her whole, and she was gone.

The silence that followed was suffocating.

Brutus spat on the floor, growling low. "Why didn't she finish it? She had us."

"Because she did not need to," Kael said, his voice tight. His hand had not left the hilt of his sword, his pulse still hammering in his ears. "She wanted us to know she is watching."

Lyra lowered her bow slowly, her eyes flicking toward the vanished dark. "And that she knew we would be here."

That thought settled heavy in the cavern. Kael turned to Thorne, searching his face. "Only me, you, Lyra, Brutus, and Thalia knew the plan for the tunnels until this morning. She should not have known."

Thorne's gaze was cold, sharp as the edge of his blade. "She knew because someone told her."

The words dropped like a stone into still water. A ripple of unease passed through the rebels, whispers rising like smoke. Kael felt their eyes on one another, suspicion and fear already creeping through the ranks.

Kael clenched his fists. "You are saying we have a traitor."

"I am saying," Thorne replied evenly, "Malrik has many claws. Some reach deeper than we think. If Veska stood here tonight, it was not chance. Someone in these tunnels walks with divided loyalty."

The rebels shifted, murmuring, their voices edged with unease. Kirros stood at the far side of the group, his face shadowed, hands tight around his spear. He did not speak.

Kael looked at the men and women around him, the faces of those who had chosen to follow him into the dark. Farmers, smiths, outcasts, and warriors alike. He thought of the boy who had handed him the wooden bird, eyes bright with faith.

The weight pressed harder.

If there was a traitor, every step forward put them closer to ruin. Yet to stop now, to turn back, would be worse. It would mean fear had already won.

Kael turned back to Thorne. "Then we find out who it is. Quietly. No panic. If Malrik thinks he has planted doubt in me, he will find I am not so easily broken."

Thorne gave a single nod, his eyes narrowing. “Good. Because the shadows ahead will test you more than any blade. And if you cannot hold your people's trust, Veska will not need to strike. They will break themselves for her.”

Kael breathed in the cold air of the cavern, letting it burn in his lungs. The path ahead was darker than ever, but there was no turning back.

He touched the wooden carving in his pocket, the bird with outstretched wings, and let its weight steady him.

Then he raised his torch, and the company pressed deeper into the veins of stone, shadows clinging to their heels and betrayal lurking unseen among them.

Chapter 17 - The Blade Mistress

The tunnels narrowed until Kael's group could only move single file. Every sound, the grind of boots against stone, the metallic rasp of a sword shifting in its sheath, echoed like a war drum in the suffocating dark. The torches gave little comfort; their flames hissed against the damp, throwing back more shadows than light.

Then came silence. Not the still quiet of empty caves, but a silence that watched them, held breath and waited.

A voice slid along the walls, cold as steel dragged over ice.

Veska, unseen from the shadows. "So... you are the prince who crawled out of the ashes. How disappointing."

Kael froze, his grip tightening around his sword. The others shifted uneasily, eyes darting to the walls, the ceiling, the black mouth of the tunnel stretching ahead. But there was no target. Only shadows that twisted like smoke, moving where the torchlight wavered.

A blur of crimson and black dropped from the ceiling. Armor traced with molten lines shimmered faintly beneath a swirl of smoke. Her mask, bone and shadowsteel, was carved into a skeletal grin, violet smoke curling from the eye slits. Kael stepped forward instinctively, blade raised.

She vanished.

In the next heartbeat, Veska appeared behind Brutus in a ripple of darkness. A black-edged blade hissed past his throat, so close it caught the edge of his tusk.

Brutus, snarling "Try that again, shadow witch!"

He swung his axe, the blow a crushing arc, but it met only stone. Veska was already gone, her armor whispering as she melted into the wall itself.

The hunt began.

She came at them in flickers. One moment at Kael's flank, the next at Lyra's back, then gone before steel could even taste her shadow. Every strike was a test, a needle-prick of speed and precision. Her movements were so fluid Kael could not track her origin until she had already faded again.

Thalia whispered quick incantations, magic flaring into radiant bursts that should have burned through shadow, but every time the light reached her, Veska bent it aside, swallowed in darkness as if the stone itself had opened its mouth.

Veska's voice echoing throughout the tunnels. "You have spirit, prince. Let me cut it from you slowly..."

This time she appeared before Kael, close, too close. He saw the hairline cracks etched across her mask, like fractures in bone. Then her blade moved, black lightning, each strike snapping faster than breath. Kael parried and deflected, sparks bursting against stone. His arms burned with the rhythm, each clash rattling bone, each swing a storm.

Brutus charged with a roar, forcing Veska to yield a step. Lyra's arrow whistled through the chaos, igniting midair as Thalia enchanted it. The shaft cut across Veska's pauldron, bursting into fire. For a moment the flames clung, not to her armor, but to the smoky veil surrounding her.

The smoke hissed away.

And for the first time, Kael saw her fully. Not a phantom, but a woman clad in crimson and black plates, every line of her armor glowing faintly as though veins of magma ran beneath.

Kael lunged.

Their swords clashed in the heart of the tunnel, the sound like a thunderclap trapped in stone.

Veska, hissing: “Better... much better.”

She spun, her blade cutting deep into Kael's shoulder. The strike seared through leather and skin, hot as poison. He stumbled back, blood soaking his tunic, his breath jagged.

Then she was gone.

Her voice echoed further down the tunnel, fading into shadow.

“You will not reach Emberdeep’s heart. Next time, I will not play.”

The silence returned, pressing heavy against stone. Only the smell of blood and smoke remained.

Kael leaned against the wall, his free hand clamped over his shoulder. Blood seeped warm between his fingers. His sword hand trembled, not with fear, but with the weight of what had just passed.

Lyra looks towards Kael. “She could have killed us.”

Kael’s jaw tightened. “She wanted to see how far we would go.”

Brutus growled low, slamming his axe against the wall in frustration. “She will bleed next time. I swear it.”

But Lyra was not looking at Brutus. She was looking at Kael, at the red slick spreading across his sleeve. Her bow was slung over her shoulder now, forgotten, as she stepped closer.

“Kael,” she said, her voice low enough that only he could hear. “Sit. Let Thalia treat it before you collapse on us.”

“I’m fine,” Kael muttered, pushing off the wall. But the pallor in his face betrayed him.

Lyra caught his wrist, firm and unyielding. “No. You are not. If you go down in front of them...” her eyes flicked to the rebels, their faces pale and shaken, “it will break them. You cannot let that happen.”

For a heartbeat Kael almost protested again, but the steel in her gaze cut deeper than Veska’s blade had. Slowly, he sank to one knee.

Thalia was already beside him, murmuring words that smelled faintly of ozone and herbs. Her hands glowed violet as she pressed against the wound, knitting flesh enough to slow the bleeding.

“It will not hold long,” she whispered. “But it will buy you time.”

Kael gritted his teeth, the pain raw but steady. He glanced up to find Lyra still watching him, her lips pressed thin, her eyes flickering with something between anger and concern.

He managed a faint smile. “I’ll live.”

“You had better,” she muttered, releasing his wrist at last.

The rebels had drawn into a loose circle, weapons ready, eyes on every shadow. One of the youngest among them, barely older than Kael himself, looked pale, his spear trembling in his grip. Another, a veteran smith with half a beard and scars from the war, muttered curses under his breath, as though swearing could keep fear away.

And near the back, Kael saw Kirros. The man's face was unreadable, his grip on his weapon steady, but his eyes darted often, first to Kael, then to the darkness where Veska had vanished.

Lyra followed his gaze. Something in her chest tightened.

She stepped closer to Kael's side. "Do you trust all of them?" she asked softly, her words meant only for him.

Kael's brow furrowed. "Why?"

"Because Veska knew. She was waiting for us here, in the tunnels." Lyra's voice dropped even lower, her tone sharper than her arrows. "And only a handful knew this plan. Someone told her."

Kael's face hardened. His shoulder throbbed, but her words cut sharper than the wound. He thought of Thorne's warning. Malrik has many claws.

His gaze slid to Kirros again, silent, shadowed, hands gripping his spear too tightly. But Kael said nothing. Not yet.

They pressed deeper into the tunnels. Every step was heavier now, burdened not only by the threat of Veska's return but by the gnawing suspicion worming its way into their ranks. Whispers passed between the rebels like disease: traitor... betrayal... Malrik's claws.

Kael kept to the front, torch raised high, blood drying stiff on his sleeve. He knew the eyes on his back were not only for protection. Some watched him with doubt now. And if doubt spread faster than flame, then Malrik had already won.

Thorne moved up beside him, his presence like a shadow of iron. "You stood your ground against her," he said, not unkindly.

Kael exhaled slowly. “Barely.”

“Barely is enough. She was testing you. And you did not break.”

Kael shook his head, his voice low. “She knew we would be here, Thorne. That was not a guess. It was not luck.”

Thorne’s single eye cut toward him, grim. “Then you already know what that means.”

Kael did not answer. His fingers brushed the wooden bird in his pocket, the gift of a child who had believed in him, who had seen him as something more than a boy with a sword. That weight steadied him as much as it burdened him.

He looked back once, rebels following in his steps. Farmers, smiths, outcasts... and somewhere among them, maybe, a traitor.

He tightened his grip on his sword.

Whether Veska returned or not, the greater battle had already begun, one fought not against shadows, but against doubt.

And if he faltered, everything could break.

The darkness pressed closer with every step, as though the tunnels themselves wanted to swallow Kael and his companions whole. The torches guttered and hissed in the damp air, their light shrinking, revealing little more than jagged walls and the gleam of moisture. The echoes of Veska’s retreat still clung to the stone, a haunting reminder that their enemy could strike at will, vanish at will, and choose the rhythm of this hunt like a wolf circling wounded prey.

Kael walked with one hand pressed to his shoulder, the blood from Veska’s cut still warm against his glove. Every jolt of pain seemed to pulse louder than the rebels’ boots. His sword arm was steady, but he could feel the weakness spreading through him like poison. He forced his steps to remain measured and strong. His men and women needed their prince to be unshaken, not bent beneath wounds.

But Lyra saw.

She kept close at his side, her bow lowered now, her eyes scanning the darkness and then darting back to him, as if she feared he might collapse without warning. Her lips parted once, twice, as if she wanted to speak, but only the soft sound of her boots came. Finally, her hand brushed his good arm, quick and fleeting.

Lyra spoke softly. “You need to stop, Kael. That wound...”

Kael shook his head, keeping his voice low but firm. “If I stop, they’ll stop. If I falter, they’ll falter. We can’t afford it.”

Her eyes searched his face, finding no give, only the hard iron of his resolve. She bit back her words, but the worry in her gaze burned brighter than the torchlight.

Behind them, the rebels trudged on, two dozen in all, though their numbers were thinner now since the clash with the Umbra scouts. Among them walked smiths with soot in their skin, farmers gripping spears with hands more used to plows, mercenaries hardened by scars, and a handful of youths whose eyes darted at every echo. One of those, Kirros, kept to the middle of the column, his spear clutched tightly, his jaw set.

Lyra’s gaze lingered on him.

He had been quiet since Veska’s appearance, too quiet. While the others muttered prayers or whispered to steady their nerves, Kirros seemed withdrawn, his eyes shadowed in thought. When he caught Lyra watching, he stiffened and looked away too quickly.

Her suspicion coiled tighter.

The tunnels forced them single file again. Brutus took the lead, his axe ready, his massive shoulders brushing against stone. Thorne followed close behind, silent, his presence heavy but grounding. He was always watchful, always gauging Kael, not only his swordplay but his judgment. Kael felt that gaze now, like a weight on the back of his neck.

The silence grew unbearable. Every drop of water sounded like an enemy's step. Every waver of the torchlight like a shadow slithering forward.

Finally, Thorne spoke, his voice deep and quiet but carrying.

"Veska doesn't miss her kill unless she means to. Tonight, she wanted us rattled. She succeeded."

Brutus grunted. "Then let her rattle. When she comes back, I'll split her mask in two."

"No," Thorne said, his tone sharp enough to cut the air. "You'll fight when the moment is right. Until then, you'll remember what every scar on your back already taught you. Underestimating her is death."

The words silenced Brutus, though his grip tightened on the axe.

Kael exhaled through his teeth. "She knew we'd be here. That wasn't chance."

He looked at his people again, and the memory of Thorne's earlier words echoed: If Veska stood here tonight, it was not chance. Someone in these tunnels walks with divided loyalty.

The paranoia was a blade turned inward, and Kael could feel it cutting his people already. The whispers were sharper now, furtive glances cast at one another. Trust was fraying, thread by thread.

Lyra's hand brushed his arm again. Her voice, barely audible: "It's Kirros."

Kael blinked, turning his head slightly toward her. "You're sure?"

"I'm not," she admitted, her lips tight. "But... he avoids me. He avoids all of us. He's too quiet. When Veska appeared, he didn't reach for his weapon until you gave the order. And when you spoke of a traitor earlier, he froze. Not like the others."

Kael glanced toward the youth, his brow furrowing. Kirros walked with his head down, the torchlight painting his features hollow. A loyal fighter, or a boy caught in the jaws of fear and guilt?

He couldn't be sure. Not yet. But suspicion was fire, and fire spread quickly.

Kael spoke low to Lyra. "Not a word to the others. If you're wrong, you'll destroy him, and we can't afford that fracture. Not now."

Her lips pressed tight, but she nodded, the tension between them sharp as a drawn bowstring.

They walked deeper.

The tunnels shifted, opening into a wider chamber. A subterranean river cut across the stone, its waters black and slow, reflecting torchlight like shattered glass. A narrow bridge of rock arched over it, slick with moss.

One of the youngest rebels, a boy barely older than the child who had given Kael the wooden bird, hesitated. His name was

Dalen, a farmer's son with more courage than skill. His hands trembled on his spear as he stared at the rushing water.

"I... I don't like this," he whispered. "Feels wrong."

Kirros placed a hand on his shoulder, steadying him. "It's just water, Dalen. Keep your eyes on the bridge, not the river." His voice was calm and steady, too steady, Lyra thought.

They crossed one by one, the air thick with the weight of imagined claws reaching from the depths. When Kael stepped onto the bridge, pain flared from his shoulder, his balance faltering. Lyra was there instantly, her hand gripping his arm, steadying him.

Her voice was sharp with worry. "You're bleeding more. You can't keep this pace."

"I have to," Kael muttered.

"Not if it kills you before Malrik does."

Their eyes met, the fire in hers clashing with the steel in his. For a moment, he nearly relented, nearly let her bind the wound, nearly admitted he was weakening. But the eyes of his soldiers were on him. To falter here, in front of them, was to plant doubt deeper than any traitor's whisper.

He pressed on.

The bridge ended, and the rebels regrouped on the far side. Their numbers smaller now, the shadows larger. Every face was strained, every movement sharper with paranoia.

Kael forced his voice to steady calm. "We're close. Emberdeep's heart lies ahead. Hold fast."

Thorne's eye narrowed, reading Kael like a page. He saw the blood, the pain, the cracks in Kael's armor. But he said nothing, only gave the faintest nod, a silent reminder that leadership was as much mask as truth.

They walked again, deeper into the bowels of stone. And with every step, Kael could feel it: their faith thinning, their suspicion growing.

When Emberdeep's heart finally came into view, it was not the living forge of legend the rebels had imagined. Once, this chamber had been the mountain's beating core, glowing veins of molten rock, the roar of eternal forges echoing like thunder.

Now it was only ruin.

The fire was gone. The vast cavern lay in darkness, its walls carved over with jagged symbols of Malrik's dominion. The markings pulsed faintly, like wounds still bleeding shadow. Where the forges had once blazed, black stone altars rose instead, cold and silent.

The rebels slowed, their breaths catching, not with awe, but with unease. The heart of Emberdeep no longer burned with life. It had been hollowed, claimed.

Kael's hand tightened on his sword. "He's poisoned even this..."

The chamber stretched wide, oppressive in its emptiness. Then, at the far side, the stone closed again. The rebels' path narrowed once more into a single, black-veined tunnel, drawing them deeper into Malrik's shadow.

Because though they had reached the next stage of their campaign, the shadows of betrayal had already walked with them into the chamber.

Kael's hand brushed the wooden bird in his pocket, its weight both anchor and burden. He looked at his people, at Lyra's watchful eyes, at Brutus's restless strength, at Thalia's quiet fire, at Thorne's unyielding steel. And then, at Kirros.

The boy's face was unreadable in the glow of the forges. Kael's jaw tightened.

The war against Malrik had reached Emberdeep. But another war, more dangerous still, had begun within.

Interlude - The Smoke Returns

The throne hall of Blackspire Keep lay in perpetual half-light, the great obsidian pillars catching only the faint glimmer of the braziers that burned with sickly green flame. Lord Malrik sat forward on his jagged throne, one gauntleted hand resting on the armrest, the other curled over the hilt of his sword. The air bent faintly around him, as though the weight of his will alone warped the space.

The braziers flickered, and the shadows behind them thickened.

From that darkness, Veska emerged. The bone-and-shadowsteel mask caught the green firelight, the faint curl of smoke trailing from her pauldrons as if she had just stepped out of another world.

She kneeled.

Malrik spit the words out with disgust. "You were tasked with ending him."

Veska Replied with a smirk. "And I could have. Many times."

Malrik's fingers drummed on the throne.

"And yet, he breathes."

Veska's tone was cool, almost amused.

"A dead prince is predictable. A living one fights harder... but the longer he runs, the more he will stumble. I've seen his limits already. His courage masks inexperience."

Malrik's eyes narrowed, but he did not interrupt. Veska rose from her kneel and paced slowly across the edge of the dais.

"He is not ready for me. Not truly. I want him to think he can face me. When I cut him down, it will break more than his body. It will shatter the will of those following him."

The green firelight caught the faintest smile beneath her mask.

Malrik gave her a look that would give others chills. "You play with prey, Veska. Do not mistake sport for strategy."

Veska bows to him. "I serve your war, Lord Malrik. My methods ensure victory, not merely battle."

For a moment, silence stretched between them. Then Malrik's gaze shifted past her, to the shadows that always followed her return.

"Very well. But next time you cross blades with him, there will be no next time."

Veska lefts her head up. "As you command."

She dissolved into smoke, the green flames dimming as her presence vanished, leaving Malrik alone, fingers still drumming, eyes fixed on the place where she had stood.

Chapter 18 - Through the Maw of Shadow

The tunnels had changed.

The air, once merely stale, now carried a damp chill that clung to skin and armor. Every footstep seemed too loud, even against the muffled dirt and stone, and every flicker of torchlight seemed to pull shadows deeper into the walls.

Kael moved at the front, sword drawn but low, his eyes flicking from one narrow passage to the next. Brutus followed close, carrying their largest torch like a miniature sun, his bulk making the tunnels feel even tighter.

Lyra's bow was in hand, an arrow notched but lowered. She kept glancing back over her shoulder, as if expecting something to crawl up from behind. Thalia walked at the rear, her violet eyes glowing faintly in the dark, magic whispering between her fingers in case she needed it instantly.

Brutus muttered. "Feels like the stone itself is watching us." Lyra quick with a response. "It is. Look at the walls."

Carved into the stone, barely visible in the torchlight, were faint etchings: jagged symbols like claws raked across rock. They were old, but freshly disturbed.

Kael stopped, raising a hand for silence. Somewhere ahead, faint and far, a sound drifted through the tunnels. Not footsteps. Not breathing.

A low, scraping whisper, like a blade dragging across stone.

Thalia grips her staff tighter. "She's still here."

No one needed to ask who she meant. Veska's presence had not been felt since the skirmish two days ago, but none of them believed she had left.

They reached a wider chamber, a place where several tunnels converged into a circular space choked with stalagmites. Kael scanned the branching paths. Each tunnel mouth looked the same.

Brutus taking lead. "Which way?"

Before Kael could answer, a sound like rushing air swept through the chamber. The torches flared, then dimmed, and smoke began curling in from all the other passages at once.

The smoke did not rise. It slithered along the floor like living ink.

A voice, soft and almost mocking, echoed from everywhere at once.

Veska like a predator chasing prey. "You have come deeper into my hunting ground, little prince. Brave... or foolish?"

Kael tightened his grip on his sword. His pulse pounded, but he kept his voice steady.

"If you want to stop me, do it now."

Silence answered him, followed by the sharp clang of steel striking stone somewhere beyond the smoke.

Lyra pulls back her bow. "She's toying with us."
Thalia spoke quietly "She's studying us."

Kael's jaw clenched. The weight of the group's eyes on him felt heavier than the sword in his hand. This was where leadership mattered, because fear could not spread.

Kael looked towards everyone. “We stay together. We keep moving. She wants us scattered. Don’t give her the chance.”

They pressed into the next tunnel, the smoke trailing them like a slow tide. Somewhere behind, the scraping sound returned, closer now.

The hunt was not over. It had only just begun.

Hours blurred together in the oppressive dark. The tunnels narrowed, widened, and narrowed again, forcing them into single file. Torches sputtered low, leaving shadows clinging to every crevice. Kael’s shoulder throbbed with every heartbeat.

When they finally paused in a small cavern to rest, Kael slumped against the wall. Lyra knelt beside him immediately, tugging at the leather straps of his armor despite his protests.

“You’re bleeding through again,” she said sharply.

“I’m fine,” Kael gritted.

“You’re not fine,” she snapped, eyes flashing. “If you bleed out before Malrik ever lays eyes on you, what then?”

Before Kael could retort, Thalia stepped forward. She held out her hand, magic flickering faintly around her fingers.

“I can tend to it,” she said quietly.

Kael looked at her, brow furrowing. “Since when do you know so much healing magic? You have always leaned toward the arcane arts of fire and light.”

Thalia’s gaze softened, almost wistful. “Because I watched. My mother was a healer, one of the best in Elaria before the wars. I used to sit beside her while she worked, memorizing her hands, her words. She wanted me to take up the craft, but I always reached for the stars and storms instead."

She knelt, setting her staff aside. "But some things stick. Enough to close wounds, if not cure the deeper hurts."

Her hands hovered over Kael's shoulder, violet glow seeping into the cut. Pain flared, then dulled. The blood slowed, the flesh knitting enough to hold.

Kael let out a breath he had not realized he was holding. "Your mother... she would be proud."

A shadow flickered in Thalia's eyes. "I hope so. She did not live long enough to see what the world became."

The silence that followed carried more weight than the stone around them.

Later, when the march resumed, Kael found himself walking beside Dalen, the young farmer's son whose hand still shook on his spear. His torchlight painted the boy's face pale.

"Dalen," Kael said softly, keeping his voice low so the others would not hear. "Why are you here?"

The boy blinked, startled by the question. "Because... because someone has to be."

Kael tilted his head. "That is not an answer."

Dalen hesitated, then sighed, his grip tightening on the spear.

"It's just me and my father now. He's older. He runs the farm, but it's harder every season. Malrik's men took our grain and livestock, left us with nothing. And then sickness took my mother and my sister."

His voice cracked. He swallowed hard.

"I couldn't just stay. I couldn't keep watching him work himself to death while I stood by. If I could help end this, if I could fight back... maybe my father could live without carrying it all alone."

Kael's chest tightened. The boy's words echoed the burden he carried himself.

"You have already honored them, just by standing here," Kael said, placing a hand briefly on the boy's shoulder. "But you will honor them more by surviving this, Dalen. Do not throw yourself away."

The boy nodded, though his eyes still burned with the fire of grief.

They pressed on until the tunnels curved into a jagged hall, stalactites hanging like teeth from the ceiling.

The scraping sound returned, louder this time, sharper, circling them. Torches flickered. Shadows moved.

And then she was there.

Veska burst from the wall itself, her mask grinning, blades flashing like black lightning. Chaos erupted.

Kael met her head-on, their swords clashing in sparks, while Brutus bellowed and swung his axe. Lyra loosed an arrow that grazed Veska's shoulder, forcing her to flicker back into the smoke.

She reappeared behind Thalia, forcing the mage to spin with a burst of violet fire. Then she was gone again, every strike a ghost, every step a whisper.

Then she appeared behind Dalen.

Her arm clamped around him, dragging him close, her blade pressed against his chest.

“This,” she hissed, her voice echoing with cruel delight, “is what it means to go against Malrik.”

“NO!” Kael roared, surging forward.

But Veska’s blade slid cleanly through Dalen’s chest. The boy gasped, eyes wide, his spear clattering to the stone.

Kael caught him before he fell, cradling him as blood spread hot across his armor.

“It’s... it’s okay,” Dalen whispered weakly, a faint smile trembling on his lips. “I can... I can see them now. My mom... and my sister...”

“No,” Kael rasped, shaking his head fiercely. “Stay with me, Dalen. Stay.”

But the boy’s eyes glazed, and his last breath slipped from his lips.

Kael’s scream tore through the cavern, raw and furious. He laid the boy gently down, closing his eyes with trembling hands.

When he rose, his rage turned like fire toward Kirros. He seized the young man by the collar, shoving him against the stone.

“I know it’s you,” Kael snarled, his voice breaking with fury. “I know you’re the traitor.”

Kirros’s face went pale. “N-no! Kael, please, I didn’t mean for this. Someone came to me the night before you arrived in

Emberdeep. They said if I told them your plans, no one would get hurt. They promised. They said they'd give me anything I wanted, a better life for my family."

"You sold us," Kael spat, shoving him harder. "You sold us to Malrik."

Tears welled in Kirros's eyes. "I thought it would keep us safe. I didn't know they'd kill..."

A voice cut him off, smooth and venomous.

"Now, now," Veska whispered from behind. Her shadow peeled from the wall, her mask grinning wide. "Malrik won't like you spilling his plans."

Before anyone could move, her blade flashed.

Kirros gasped as the shadowsteel slit his throat, blood spilling hot across the stone. His body crumpled at Kael's feet.

Veska's laugh echoed like broken glass before she vanished into the dark once more.

The tunnel chamber reeked of blood and smoke. Kirros's body slumped against the cold stone, his lifeless eyes still wide with the shock of betrayal, and of Veska's blade silencing him forever. The shadows that had delivered her drifted apart like smoke in a breeze, leaving only the rasp of unsteady breathing among the rebels.

For a long, terrible moment, no one moved.

Kael stood frozen, his sword trembling in his hand. First Dalen, torn from them with merciless cruelty. Then Kirros, whose cowardice had cost them dearly, and yet whose death had been claimed before Kael's justice could fall. Veska had stolen even that from him.

Brutus's growl filled the silence. He planted his axe into the stone floor with a sharp crack.

"Damn her! She's making sport of us."

Lyra's voice was quieter, but every word carried the sting of iron. "And now she knows what we'll do before we do it. Kirros told her more than once. He sold us all for a promise."

Murmurs spread through the rebels, anger, fear, and despair mixing in the chamber's cold air.

The walls seemed to lean closer. Some turned their eyes on Kael, seeking direction. Others looked away, afraid of what they might see.

Kael drew a slow, steadying breath. He sheathed his blade, not because the fight was done, but because his people needed their leader more than his fury. He forced his voice to rise above the ragged quiet.

Kael yelled out. "Enough."

The word echoed off the stone. The murmurs fell still.

Kael's gaze swept the group, sharp and unyielding. "Veska wanted this. She wanted to break us before Malrik ever needed to raise his hand. She wanted us turning on each other, doubting, splintering. She thinks she's already won."

He stepped forward, kneeling briefly by Dalen's body. The boy's eyes were still half-lidded, his lips parted as though he might yet speak. Kael closed them gently, his fingers tightening for a moment on Dalen's brow. When he rose, his voice rang louder, hard as steel:

“But she is wrong. Dalen was one of us. He bled for this cause. And though Kirros chose poorly, his betrayal ended. No more will follow. Do you hear me? No more.”

The rebels stirred, voices muttering back, first uncertain, then firm, until a rough chorus answered him.

Thalia’s soft voice followed. “Kael is right. If we falter now, Veska’s blade has already cut deeper than any wound we see. The shadows want fear. We must give them defiance instead.”

Kael nodded, gratitude flickering in his eyes toward her.

Then he looked to Brutus. “We bury Dalen here. He deserves rest, not to be left for the shadows.”

Brutus grunted, already moving to his side, shoulders tensed. “Aye. I’ll see it done.”

The rebels set to work. Torches burned low as stone and earth were cleared from a recess in the cavern floor. They laid Dalen down carefully, wrapping him in spare cloth. Some whispered prayers, others only bowed their heads. The scrape of stone against stone was the only sound for a time.

Kael remained by the grave until the last stone was placed. His hand lingered on the hilt of his sword, the weight of command pressing heavier than ever.

Lyra stepped beside him. Her voice was low, meant for him alone. “He believed in you. Right until the end. Don't let her twist that into weakness.”

Kael’s jaw tightened. “I won't. Dalen’s blood, Kirros’s betrayal, it all ends with Malrik. I swear it.”

He turned back to the others, lifting his torch high. His voice was iron, unbroken:

“We move forward. Emberdeep’s tunnel’s end is close, and with it the chance to strike back. For Dalen. For every soul Malrik thinks he owns. We are not shadows, we are fire. And we will burn his reign to ash.”

The rebels, shaken but steadied, answered with a rising roar. Their voices carried through the tunnels, defying the dark.

As they pressed onward, Kael walked at the front again, his wound fully mended thanks to Thalia's skill, but his heart carrying fresh scars. Behind him, the rebels followed, bound tighter by loss, rage, and a vow none would let die.

Yet in the silence between footfalls, Kael's thoughts whispered of Veska’s grin, of her promise that next time she would not play.

And he swore to himself that when that next time came, he would not run. He would not falter.

He would end her.

Chapter 19 - Predator in the Deep

The tunnels narrowed before widening again into a cavern chamber where the air shifted, cooler, thinner, fresher. They were close now, close to the surface, close to the end of Emberdeep's suffocating labyrinth. Kael could feel it with every breath, the weight of stone lifting little by little.

But the shadows had followed them every step.

Kael raised his hand, halting the group. Torchlight danced against the walls, revealing the raw faces of those who remained. Seven rebels, tired, battered, but alive. Men and women who had seen friends fall and who had pushed past fear until only iron resolve remained. Behind them came Brutus, axe heavy across his broad shoulders; Lyra, bow half drawn even in stillness; Thalia, pale with exhaustion but her hands glowing faintly; and Thorne, the old general whose presence was like bedrock beneath their feet.

Kael breathed deep. His wound from Veska's last ambush was healed, Thalia's magic leaving only a faint ache. But grief pressed heavier than steel. Dalen's face still haunted him, silenced forever by Veska's cruelty. Kirros's betrayal lingered, a bitter echo.

He looked over his people. Their eyes searched his, waiting. He would not let them see doubt.

"Stay close," Kael whispered. "No stragglers. If she comes, we hold formation. Together."

Brutus grunted. "If she comes? Boy, she's already here."

Kael opened his mouth to answer, but then the air shifted.

A voice slithered through the stone.

"You have crawled far, little prince."

Veska stepped from the shadows as though born from them. Her crimson and black armor rippled with smoke, twin blades gleaming in the torchlight. The predator's mask tilted toward him, its bone-white grin frozen and merciless.

Behind her, the Umbra Legions materialized, dozens of shadow-forged warriors, half smoke, half steel, their red eyes burning with malice. They lined the cavern walls like a tide ready to break.

One of the rebels muttered a curse. Another whispered a prayer.

Kael lifted his sword. His voice carried steady, unyielding. "Then let this be where you fall."

Veska's laugh was low and cruel. "Oh no, prince. This is where I make you beg."

With a flick of her wrist, the Legions surged.

The cavern exploded into battle.

The seven rebels roared, charging shoulder to shoulder into the wave of shadows. Steel clanged, and torches scattered sparks. For every Umbra struck down, two more seemed to form from smoke and fire.

Kael met the first blow head-on, his sword cleaving through a soldier's smoky chest. The body dissolved with a hiss, reforming at the edge of the torchlight. He pivoted, blade flashing, cutting another before it could strike Thalia.

To his right, Brutus was a storm. His axe smashed through shadow after shadow, each swing tearing the air apart. He bellowed curses at them, his voice thunderous. Yet the shadows pressed him, spears darting, blades scraping sparks from his armor.

Lyra shot arrow after arrow, her shots glowing faintly with ember-crystal dust. Each shaft burned through the shadows, scattering them to mist. She shifted positions constantly, weaving between rebels, her bowstring never silent.

Thalia stood at the center, hands raised. Her barriers shimmered like glass domes, flickering each time an Umbra weapon struck. Sweat poured down her pale cheeks, her voice steady as she whispered the incantations to hold the shields together.

And Thorne was iron. His great sword swung in clean, perfect arcs, cutting swaths through the enemy. His voice rose above the clash, sharp as a whip.

"Ryo, shield right. Lyra, cover the flank. Brutus, step back, you will overextend."

His commands pulled chaos into order, his presence turning desperation into defense.

Veska watched at first, circling the edges like a predator. Every step she took, Kael felt it, her gaze locked on him, hungry and cruel. She wanted him to break.

And Kael was ready.

The seven rebels fought with everything left in them.

Eran, a wiry man with a jagged scar down his cheek, slammed his shield into an Umbra, driving his spear through its head before it could reform. "For Dalen," he roared, the cry picked up by two others near him.

Marra, a former mason with arms thick as stone, swung her hammer with brutal strength, shattering shadowsteel into smoke. Blood ran from her brow, but her teeth were bared in a grim smile.

Two brothers, Ryo and Leo, fought back to back, their blades flashing in the torchlight. They had grown up in the mines beneath Emberdeep, swinging picks long before they ever swung swords, and now they fought like men trying to carve their home back from hell itself.

The Umbra pressed hardest at their flank, shadows writhing and blades whispering death. Leo caught one across the chest, grunting as he shoved it back, while Ryo parried another that lunged from the dark.

"Stay with me, brother," Ryo shouted, his voice cracking with strain.

Leo smiled through blooded lips. "Wouldn't dream of—"

The words cut off as a blade slid through his ribs. His eyes went wide, breath catching in a soundless gasp. Ryo's scream tore through the chamber, raw and ragged, as Leo crumpled to his knees.

Ryo lunged forward, fury blinding him, hacking down the Umbra that struck his brother. He dragged Leo's body back with trembling arms, planting himself before him like a wall, stabbing again and again into the encroaching dark.

"Come on, then," he roared. "Come and take him from me."

The Umbra swarmed, but Ryo's blade sang. Each swing was vengeance, each breath defiance. Around him, Kael's voice rose, rallying the others to hold the line as the tunnels shook with the clash of steel and shadow.

Every breath, every strike, was survival bought with pain. Yet none faltered. Not with Kael before them, not with Veska watching.

Then the air shifted. The shadows thinned for a moment, and Veska struck.

She dropped from the ceiling in a blur, blades flashing, landing before Kael with a predator's grace.

Steel rang as their swords clashed. Sparks lit the chamber. Veska pressed him, her movements liquid, every strike flowing into the next. Kael parried, his arms shaking from the force, sweat stinging his eyes.

She hissed through her mask. "Does his scream still echo in your ears, prince? The boy's? So small. So fragile. Did you watch him die?"

Kael's fury surged. He shoved forward, his sword hammering against hers. "I'll kill you for him. One day, Veska. For Dalen, I will end you."

Her laugh was sharp and cruel. "Then show me, little prince."

Their duel raged. Kael struck high, low, to the side, forcing her back. But Veska was fast, faster than thought, her blades darting like fangs. One slash slipped past his guard, nicking his cheek. Another tore through his sleeve, grazing his arm.

Then she spun, one blade cutting wide, and it struck Brutus as he cut down an Umbra at Kael's flank.

The axe man staggered, blood spraying from his side. He bellowed but did not fall, clutching the wound as he swung his axe with his other hand.

Kael's heart lurched. "Brutus."

But Brutus snarled, teeth bared. "Fight, boy! Don't you dare stop now!

Kael turned back just in time to block Veska's killing blow. Their blades locked, sparks flying, her mask inches from his face.

"Too slow," she hissed.

"Not slow enough," Kael spat, and drove his sword upward in a sudden burst.

Kael's strike came like lightning, clean, deliberate, driven by every ounce of rage he had buried since Dalen's death.

The blade tore through the swirl of shadows guarding Veska's flank and bit deep across her right side, slicing through armor and flesh alike.

Veska's eyes widened in real shock as she staggered back, her breath catching. Dark blood spilled, hissing where it struck the stone. For the first time, her poise faltered; the predator had been wounded.

Kael leveled his sword at her, chest heaving. "That is for Dalen."

Veska looked down at her blood-slick side, then up at him, her lips curving into a small, cold smile. "So the cub has teeth after all."

She took a slow step back, the air around her rippling with shadow. "Remember this, little prince. A wound shared is a tether. When next we meet, you will feel this cut as I do, and it will burn from the inside."

Her form began to dissolve, darkness peeling away like smoke.

Kael lunged forward, but the tip of his sword met only air. Veska's last words lingered, echoing through the cavern as the shadows vanished:

"The next time we meet, you will know which of us truly bleeds."

The Umbra faltered with her. Their forms flickered, weaker, slower. The rebels seized the moment, surging forward. Eran speared one through the chest. Marra's hammer shattered another. Lyra loosed her final arrow, striking a shadow through the head before it dissolved into smoke.

Brutus, bleeding heavily, crushed one last Umbra beneath his axe, his roar shaking the cavern.

Shadows surged around the remaining. Smoke curled, swallowing them. In an instant, the cavern was empty of enemies, silent except for the rasp of labored breathing.

Kael stood frozen, sword trembling in his hand. His chest heaved, sweat and blood staining him. Veska's wound replayed in his mind, her retreat burning into memory.

Behind him, Brutus collapsed to one knee, a hand clamped over his side. Blood seeped between his fingers, dark and heavy against the flickering light.

Thalia stumbled toward him, exhaustion written in every motion. Her palms glowed faintly, the shimmer of healing magic flickering like a dying ember. She pressed them to his wound, whispering an incantation under her breath, her voice trembling.

For a moment, the glow brightened. The bleeding slowed. But then her magic faltered, dimming as her shoulders sagged. She gasped softly, sweat beading on her brow.

“Come on. Just a little more,” she whispered, forcing the light to return, but it sputtered and died again. Her body simply could not give any more.

Brutus caught her wrist, his voice rough but steady. “Enough, lass. You have done what you can.”

“But it is not closing.”

“I said enough,” he rumbled, cutting her off gently. He tore a strip of cloth from his cloak and pressed it to the wound, wrapping it tight around his side. “I will live. Takes more than a shadow witch's knife to finish me.”

Thalia’s eyes glimmered with guilt, but Brutus gave her a faint grin through the pain. “Save your strength. We will need it yet.”

Kael turned toward them, watching the faint tremor in Thalia’s hands, the toll of her magic plain. His jaw set. They had all bled tonight, in body and in spirit.

Lyra dropped her bow at last, her shoulders shaking with exhaustion. Thorne leaned on his great sword, scanning the shadows with wary eyes.

The seven rebels, now five, two lost in the clash, stood bloodied but alive. Their eyes turned to Kael, searching, waiting.

Kael raised his sword high, his voice iron and unbroken.

"She runs. She bleeds. She knows we will not break. For Dalen, for every soul Malrik thinks his, we will see this through. Do you hear me?"

The rebels answered, voices ragged but fierce. A roar that filled the cavern.

Kael lowered his blade. His eyes burned with grief and with vengeance yet unclaimed.

In the silence, he whispered for himself alone, "One day, Veska. One day, I will end you."

Interlude - The Predator's Oath

The world beyond Emberdeep's lower tunnels was not much kinder than the depths.
The air was colder here, sharper, tinged with the acrid bite of brimstone from the volcanic vents. Veska moved like a wounded animal, her steps silent but slower than usual. Every heartbeat sent a pulse of pain through her side where Kael's blade had found her.

The shadows she usually commanded so effortlessly now clung to her in ragged tatters, flickering at the edges like dying embers. She hated the weakness, hated the memory of his strike replaying in her mind.

When the obsidian doors to Malrik's chamber loomed ahead, she pushed them open without ceremony. The throne room was a cavern of black stone and crimson banners, lit by a single massive brazier whose flames burned the color of blood.

Lord Malrik sat at the far end, his armored frame hunched like a vulture over a clutch of maps and war tokens. His eyes, cold, predatory, and glinting faintly red, lifted at her approach.

"You're late." His voice was deep, unhurried, dangerous.

Veska stopped a few paces away and removed her mask. The predator's skull visage fell away to reveal a face pale from blood loss, her eyes still sharp despite the pain. The gash along her side was hastily wrapped, but dark stains seeped through the bandages.

"I engaged the prince." Her tone was even, but there was a roughness to it, a forced control. "Tested his formation. Harassed his group through the tunnels. They fought well under pressure."

Malrik's gaze narrowed. "And yet you bleed."

Veska's lips curled in the faintest smirk. "Yes. He marked me."

With slow deliberation, she peeled back the edge of her armor, revealing the wound in full. It was clean but deep, a diagonal cut that would scar even with perfect healing. The flesh around it was angry and raw.

Malrik leaned back in his throne, a low hum in his throat. "Interesting. Few men can land a blow on you."

"He's not his father," Veska said, voice low. "But there is a spark in him. Something dangerous. I thought I would break him quickly. I was mistaken."

Malrik's eyes glinted with something that might have been approval or amusement. "And what do you intend to do with this mistake?"

Veska's hand went to the wound, fingers curling over it like a vow. "I will carry this mark until I return it, deeper and in his heart. The next time I face him, I will not be testing him. I will be ending him."

For a moment, silence hung heavy between them, broken only by the slow crackle of the brazier's flame.

Malrik finally spoke, his voice quiet but iron edged. "Good. Let the scar remind you. And let him feel the weight of what he has awakened."

Veska replaced her mask, the bone-white visage seeming even more sinister in the dim light. She bowed once, short and sharp, and turned to leave. Her steps were steady now, pain ignored.

The hunt was not over. It had only just begun.

Backstory - Mistress of the Shadowsteel Blades

Origin

Veska was born in the forsaken borderlands between Elaria and the Shrouded Marshes, a region where famine, raiders, and mercenaries made survival a curse. Her village was a hunting ground for every invading force, and her earliest memory was hiding under blood-soaked floorboards while soldiers butchered her family.

When she was taken as a child-slave by a passing warlord, she learned quickly that weakness was death. She killed her first man at ten, her master at twelve, and by sixteen she had already carved a reputation as a phantom assassin.

It was during those years that she began to forge her mask, fashioned from the bones of her slain master and bound with fragments of shadowsteel, a rare cursed ore that fuses with living flesh. When she placed it on, it became part of her, whispering with the voices of the slain and feeding on her cruelty.

The Oath to Malrik

Veska came into Malrik's service long before he became king. When Malrik was still consolidating his rebellion against the royal line, he needed someone to purge the shadows: spies, deserters, and hidden strongholds that refused his banners. Veska was his answer.

He promised her what no one else had: freedom through fear. Her payment would not be gold or titles, but the right to carve her name into history as the unseen executioner of kingdoms. She agreed, and with his dark blessing, she became the first commander of the Umbra Legions, a regiment of killers trained in silence, deception, and shadow-forged weapons.

Her Philosophy
Veska has no loyalty to crown or bloodline, only to the art of fear. She believes that terror is the purest form of control, more enduring than love or law. "A man who loves you may betray you. A man who fears you obeys until death."

She views Malrik as the only man who truly understands that truth. But her loyalty is not without edges: she obeys because he gave her purpose, not because she cannot dream of betrayal.

Personality
Cold, calculating, with a twisted sense of humor.
Speaks little in public, preferring her mask and silence to do the talking.
In private, she taunts, challenges, and even mocks Malrik, but always in a way that suggests admiration wrapped in cruelty.
Her bond with the Umbra Legions is almost maternal: she trains them as killers but calls them her children of silence.
Many would follow her over Malrik if it came to it.

The Scar
Her defeat in Emberdeep marks her first true failure in years. Kael's blade, breaking through her smoke and speed, left her with a deep wound along her side. For the first time, Veska bleeds not for a job or a lesson, but from being bested in honest combat.

The scar becomes both her obsession and her vow. She refuses to let it heal cleanly, instead binding it with shadowsteel to keep it visible, a permanent reminder of Kael. In her words:

"Scars are the only truth. They do not lie, they do not fade. His sword has given me mine. Next, I will give him his."

Chapter 20 - Scars in the Dark

The silence that followed was almost worse than the battle.

Shadows still clung to the walls of the tunnels, wavering like smoke, remnants of Veska's power that refused to die even after she had fled. Kael stood in the center of the ruined chamber, his sword hanging limply at his side, the blade streaked with a dark ichor that did not gleam like blood but drank the torchlight into itself. His chest rose and fell in ragged breaths, sweat matting his hair against his forehead. Every muscle in his body trembled as if some invisible weight pressed down on him.

They had survived, but only barely.

"Kael..." Lyra's voice broke the silence, hushed and unsteady. She stood a few steps away, one hand pressed against her ribs where Veska's blade had cut too close. Her eyes, usually quick with sharp words and defiance, were wide with a mixture of awe and fear. Not of him, but of what they had endured.

Behind her, Brutus leaned heavily against the tunnel wall, his massive frame slumped as though the earth itself was the only thing holding him upright. Blood streaked his arm from shoulder to elbow, and though he tried to hide it with a grunt, his breathing was uneven and shallow.

Thalia sat cross-legged on the ground a little further away, her staff lying across her knees. Violet light flickered weakly around her hands, sparks of magic trying and failing to gather. She looked pale, her lips pressed thin in frustration at her own exhaustion.

And Thorne... the old general stood apart from them all, arms folded across his chest, gaze fixed on Kael with a weight that was harder to bear than the tunnel's silence.

Kael swallowed, forcing his voice to remain steady. "She's gone."

"For now," Thalia muttered bitterly, her tone thin and hoarse. "But she'll be back. They don't retreat without reason."

Lyra gave her a sharp glance but said nothing. She simply shifted closer to Kael, the fingers of her free hand brushing against his as if to remind him he was not standing there alone.

Kael looked at her briefly, then down at the sword in his hand. The shadow-blood clinging to the blade pulsed faintly, like dying embers. He tightened his grip before sliding it back into its sheath with a hollow scrape.

For a long time, no one moved. The tunnels felt like a tomb.

They could not risk pressing further in their condition, so they withdrew into one of Emberdeep's side tunnels. Brutus had argued at first, his pride unwilling to stop while enemies still lingered in the dark, but even he could not deny his wounds.

The fire they built sputtered and crackled, its glow weak against the suffocating stone walls. Still, it was warmth, and warmth was enough.

Kael sat near the flames, staring into them without really seeing. His armor was stripped away in pieces beside him, dented and scarred. The weight of it all, battle, leadership, survival, pressed down until he wondered if he might shatter beneath it.

Lyra sat across from him, her bow unstrung, her hair falling in damp strands around her face. She was tending her side with careful movements, but every time the bandage tightened, she flinched and hissed softly.

"You fought well today," she said suddenly, her voice carrying across the fire.

Kael blinked, dragging his eyes from the flames to her. "We almost died."

Lyra tilted her head, her expression unreadable in the flickering light. "That doesn't mean you didn't fight well."

Kael shook his head. "If I were truly a leader, I would have kept you all safe. I nearly led us into death."

Brutus let out a low rumble from where he lay stretched out nearby, his massive frame rising and falling with each breath. "Bah. You think any leader can promise safety? Foolish thought. Battle always takes its due."

"Brutus is right," Thalia murmured, her violet eyes half-closed as she leaned against the wall. "Magic itself demands balance. Power never comes without cost. You..." she hesitated, then fixed Kael with a steady gaze, "you carried that cost for us today. That is what made the difference."

Kael clenched his fist. Their words felt like knives. He wanted to accept them, but his heart rebelled, whispering that he had not done enough, that his blade had faltered, that his command had wavered.

Lyra leaned forward, her hand brushing against his across the ground between them. Her touch was light but firm, pulling his gaze back to her. "You are not supposed to be perfect, Kael. You are supposed to endure. That is what we follow."

The words sank deep, lingering in the silence that followed. For the first time since Veska's retreat, Kael drew a slow, steady breath.

When the others drifted into uneasy rest, Thorne remained awake, standing at the edge of the camp with his back to the wall. His eyes were sharp even in the dim glow of the fire, watching Kael as the young man sat, sword resting across his knees.

The old general's thoughts churned like a storm. He remembered the night he had carried Kael from the burning palace, the cries of a murdered king echoing through his ears. He remembered the boy's small frame trembling in his arms, the weight of destiny thrust upon him before he could even understand it.

And now... here he was. Not a boy anymore. Not quite a man either, but something forged in between, hammered by loss and battle into a shape that was neither fragile nor complete.

The boy saved that night is gone. Thorne thought bitterly, his jaw tight. *What stands here now is something else. Something the world will have to reckon with.*

For the first time, Thorne felt both pride and fear in equal measure.

Sleep did not last long. Emberdeep's tunnels had their own voices, whispers that curled through the air like smoke. At first Kael thought he dreamed them, but when he stirred awake, he saw Thalia sitting upright, her violet eyes narrowed, staff clutched tightly.

"They're watching us," she whispered, her voice trembling. "Remnants of the Umbra Legion. They linger, feeding on the shadow, waiting for weakness."

Brutus stirred, his hand falling to the axe beside him. Lyra rose silently, her bow strung in an instant despite her wounds.

Kael stood, drawing his sword with deliberate calm. The blade gleamed faintly, hungry for battle, though Kael felt none of its hunger in his own heart. Only resolve.

"Then we move," he said. His voice carried authority now, steadier than before. "No more waiting."

Together, they pressed through the tunnels once more, shadows trailing like wolves.

The journey to the surface was grueling. Every step was weighed down by exhaustion, every turn haunted by echoes of Veska's power. Yet Kael led them without faltering, his voice steady, his pace measured. Where once he might have doubted himself, now he carried their trust like a shield.

When at last the pale light of dawn spilled through a jagged crack in the stone, they staggered into it like survivors of a shipwreck crawling onto shore.

Kael was the last to step out, pausing at the mouth of the tunnel. Behind him, Emberdeep yawned wide and black, its shadows clinging like chains. He turned, staring into that abyss one final time.

"If scars are truth," he whispered under his breath, words meant only for himself, "then let mine be for Elaria."

His hand brushed the hilt of his sword, and he stepped into the light.

Far above them, unseen, a raven cut through the morning sky. Its wings beat with unnatural rhythm, eyes gleaming with a faint, malignant glow. It circled once, watching the battered group leave Emberdeep, then turned sharply toward the east.

Toward Malrik's throne. The news of their survival would not remain a secret.

Interlude – Brutus, the Last of Ironhide

The fire crackled low, throwing long shadows across the hollow where Kael's band had taken shelter. The night was still, too still, with only the whisper of wind among the rocks and the quiet clink of Thorne sharpening his blade. Lyra sat with her bow across her knees, gaze distant, while Thalia busied herself with a satchel of herbs.

Brutus sat apart from them, as he always did, a hulking silhouette against the glow. His massive shoulders were hunched, his tusked jaw shadowed, eyes fixed on the embers as though searching for something in their depths.

Kael watched him. He had grown used to Brutus's booming laughter, to the way the orc filled silence with jokes and bravado as easily as he swung his axe. But tonight his humor was gone, his voice absent, and an unusual heaviness clung to him like a storm pressing against the edges of their little fire.

"Brutus," Kael said at last, his voice quiet but steady. "What weighs on you?"

The orc did not move at first. Then, slowly, he reached into the pouch at his side. When he pulled his hand free, something glinted in the firelight: a jagged shard of blackened steel, the broken head of an axe. He held it with surprising gentleness for hands so scarred.

"This," Brutus rumbled, his voice low as a distant drum, "was my father's."

The others stilled. Thorne's blade paused mid-stroke. Lyra's eyes flicked toward him, sharp and curious. Thalia's hands froze over her herbs.

Kael leaned forward, sensing the weight of what was coming.

Brutus drew a long breath. "I was born to the Ironhide Clan. We lived in the Stonefang Mountains, where winters cut like knives and the sky is always gray. My people were strong, bound by blood and oath. We were not raiders, as men called us. We were guardians of our own. Our walls held against beast and storm alike."

His deep voice softened, touched with memory. "My father, Rorgath Ironhide, was our chieftain. A giant of a warrior, feared in battle, yet his laughter could shake snow from the trees. My mother kept the hearth. My brothers fought beside our father, their backs scarred, their voices proud. And I... I was the youngest. Not yet tested."

For a fleeting moment, there was warmth in his expression, a flicker of the boy he had once been. But it vanished quickly, buried beneath shadow.

"It ended in fire," he said. His hand clenched around the shard of steel. "One winter, when the passes were snow-choked and we thought ourselves safe, they came. Malrik's soldiers, men, goblins, beasts. Led by betrayal. Someone sold our home for gold."

Kael's breath caught. Lyra's jaw tightened; she knew betrayal all too well.

"They fell upon us at night. My father fought like the storm itself, my brothers beside him. My mother put a hammer in my hands and told me to stand. I tried." His eyes flicked to Kael, then away. "But I was only a boy. Strong, but untested. I saw my father pierced by a dozen spears, still dragging men into the grave with him. My brothers cut down one by one. My mother..."

The words faltered, his tusked jaw tightening. His gaze returned to the broken steel. "She shoved me into a hidden tunnel, though she was already bleeding. The last thing I heard was her scream as the stone collapsed. And when I crawled out on the other side, there was nothing left of Grath'kul Hold but fire on the wind."

Silence pressed down on them all. The fire popped, the only sound.

Kael's heart clenched. He saw himself in Brutus's words: the flames, the helplessness, the crushing weight of survival when all else was ash.

"What did you do?" Kael asked quietly.

"I wandered," Brutus said. "Half-dead, carrying this." He lifted the axe-head again. "The last piece of my father. Wolves stalked me. Hunger gnawed me. But I did not die. I was found by mercenaries. They healed me, not out of kindness, but because they saw what I could become. I grew among them, fought among them, learned the ways of killing not for honor, but for coin."

He spat the last word like poison.

"I became their beast. Their shield. Their monster. And yet... every night, when the battle din was quiet, I would sit apart. And whisper the names of my family, so they would not fade from the world. That was all I carried. That, and this shard of steel."

Thorne bowed his head slightly, as if in respect. Lyra's eyes softened, the usual sharpness dulled by shared understanding of loss. Thalia's lip trembled, though she said nothing.

“And then,” Brutus said, his gaze lifting to Kael at last, “I met you. A boy, too small for his blade, too stubborn to bow.

You had lost everything, as I had. But where I sought only survival, you sought justice. A crown. A future. In you, I saw not just a cause, but a kinship. You are what my people might have become, had they lived. And so, I swore myself.”

Kael swallowed hard. His throat felt tight, chest heavy. “Brutus...”

The orc rumbled deep in his chest, almost a laugh, though it was without mirth. “Do not pity me, Kael. My clan died, but their spirit endures. Every time I fight beside you, I hear them again. Every time I shield you, I honor the shield they once tried to be for me. This is my path. My choice.”

He looked down at the shard one last time, then closed his fist around it. “If I fall, so be it. But let my fall buy you the breath to rise.”

The fire guttered low, shadows long across his scarred face. None spoke for a long while. What words could be offered in the face of such truth?

At last, Kael found his voice. “You will not fall. Not while I still stand. I swear it.”

Brutus looked at him then, and for the first time in Kael’s memory, there was something almost like peace in the orc’s eyes.

Chapter 21 – Ashes of the Wound

The sunlight felt strange.

After days of choking stone and shadows in Emberdeep, the open sky stretched like an ocean above them, endless, raw, and blindingly bright. The group staggered from the cavern mouth into the foothills, boots sinking into soft earth that smelled faintly of grass and ash.

For a long while, no one spoke. Each breath seemed to remind them they were still alive, though life itself felt thin and borrowed.

Kael shielded his eyes with a trembling hand, his fingers still bandaged from where Veska's blade had nearly taken them. The wound had healed cleanly, but the ache remained, a memory of shadowsteel that refused to fade. He forced himself to stand tall, to meet the world not as a survivor crawling out of the dark, but as a leader stepping into the light.

Behind him, Brutus lumbered with his axe slung across his back, moving heavily, each step a war between will and pain. The bandage around his side was dark with fresh stain. Thalia stayed near, violet eyes narrowed, her fingers faintly glowing as if she could hold his strength together with sheer magic.

Lyra walked apart, her bow slung, gaze scanning the ridgelines. The sun caught her hair like tarnished copper as her eyes moved constantly, searching the hills for any sign of pursuit.

Only Thorne seemed steady. The old general brought up the rear, calm and quiet, every motion measured. His eyes were deep-set beneath his helm, watching the boy he had once carried as an infant now walk like a man haunted by every shadow that had ever reached for him.

They did not speak until the cavern mouth behind them had shrunk to a wound in the mountain.

"Air feels different," Brutus muttered at last, his voice hoarse. He coughed, wiping his mouth with the back of his hand. His skin looked pale, almost gray, as though the mountain had leached the color from him.

Kael slowed, glancing back. "You alright?"

Brutus grunted. "I've had worse." But his step faltered, and Thalia's frown deepened.

Kael turned to the rest of the group, five rebels who had survived the tunnels with them. Exhausted, bloodied, faces smudged with soot and fear, yet their eyes burned with that stubborn spark that refused to die.

He drew a folded, half-burned map from his cloak. The parchment was creased and dirt-stained, the ink fading but legible enough.

"We can't all move together," he said quietly, kneeling in the dirt. He spread the map on a flat rock, weighing it with his dagger. "We're too exposed in the open. Veska's still alive, and Malrik's scouts will be hunting for anyone who made it out of Emberdeep."

The rebels gathered closer, huddling around the map. Kael pointed to a small mark just east of their position. "There's a village here. Dunhollow. It's small, and if reports I read before we left are right, it still holds a healer. Go there. Rest. Get your wounds seen to."

One of the rebels, a young woman named Sera, shook her head. "We should stay with you my lord. You'll need every blade."

Kael raised a hand, cutting her off, not in anger but in resolve. "Sera, listen to me. You five are the last of Emberdeep's fighters who made it back with us. That means you carry more than swords. You carry proof that we still stand. When the time comes, you'll return to Emberdeep and show them we still have a fighting chance. That the crown's flame isn't gone yet."

Sera's throat tightened. She looked at him as if wanting to argue, but the weight in his words stilled her.

Kael softened, a faint, weary smile crossing his face. "And please... don't call me lord. Not yet. Just Kael."

Sera nodded slowly, voice low. "Alright, Kael. We'll see it done."

He looked to each of them in turn, Sera, Ryo, Marra, Eran, and Kester. They bore their fatigue like armor, faces hollowed but eyes defiant. Scarred, bruised, and bound together by a war that had taken everything yet still refused to end.

Kael continued, "Once you're healed, take this route." His finger traced the edge of the mountains. "Head toward the Witherlands. We'll regroup there. Thorne and I will make contact when the path is safe."

Thorne stepped forward then, nodding in approval. "He's right. The Witherlands have ruins deep enough to hide an army. Go, rest, mend, and wait for the signal."

The five rebels looked between one another, then at Kael. For a long moment, none spoke. Then Ryo bowed his head. "We'll see you again, my lord. My apologies, Kael. That's a promise."

Kael clasped his shoulder. "Make sure you do. I'll need you when we take back the crown."

With that, they parted. The five rebels set out eastward, vanishing over the ridge one by one, until their silhouettes were swallowed by sunlight and distance.

Kael watched them go, the map still clutched in his hand, and for a brief, unguarded moment, he felt the weight of every life depending on him.

Lyra stepped up beside him, folding her arms. “Sending them away won't make the burden lighter.”

“No,” Kael said quietly, folding the map. “But it might keep them alive long enough to matter.”

By midday, the sun burned high and hot, and they found a low ridge where grass bent in the wind. Kael called for a halt.

They dropped their packs, breathing hard. Brutus lowered himself with a grunt, and a sharp hiss escaped his teeth. His hand went to his side.

Kael knelt beside him. “Let me see.”

“I said I'm fine,” Brutus growled, but his pallor betrayed him. Thalia ignored the protest, pulling the bandage away, and gasped. Black veins webbed outward from the gash, spreading beneath the skin like cracks in glass.

“Shadow-venom,” she murmured. “It’s spreading fast.”

Kael's stomach twisted. “Can you cleanse it?”

Thalia shook her head, voice barely above a whisper. “Not without rest. Not without focus. My magic’s stretched thin already.”

Brutus caught her hand, grinning through the pain. “You worry too much. I’ll live long enough to swing this axe again.”

Lyra muttered something under her breath that sounded suspiciously like, “Stubborn fool.”

They made camp that night on the edge of the foothills, where grass gave way to blackened earth. Despite Lyra’s protests about drawing attention, Kael insisted on a fire.

“If something comes, we’ll face it. We need warmth. And light.” He meant more than flames.

The fire cracked, painting their faces in restless gold. Brutus sat propped against a log, jaw tight, the veins at his side darkening. Thalia sat beside him, hands faintly glowing as she whispered what little healing she could summon. Lyra perched a few feet away, spinning an arrow between her fingers, her eyes reflecting the firelight.

Kael sat across from her. “You’ve been quiet,” he said.

She smirked faintly. “And you've been loud with your orders and speeches.”

“Too loud?”

Her smirk softened. “You carry every loss like it’s yours alone. Emberdeep, Dalen, Kirros. You wonder if you’re leading them to hope or ruin.”

Kael looked into the fire. “I wonder if I’m turning into Malrik.”

Lyra’s voice was gentle now. “The fact that you ask that means you’re not.”

He looked up at her, firelight catching her eyes. “You believe in me?”

“I wouldn’t still be here if I didn’t.”

For a long time, there was only the sound of crackling wood and the low hum of Thalia's exhausted chanting.

Thorne sat apart, his sword across his knees, eyes half-closed but mind alert. He had seen this before, the moment after survival when soldiers either hardened or broke. Kael was still deciding which he would be.

Dawn came grey and cold.

By the second hour, they reached the ruins of a village nestled in the valley below, a place Kael had seen marked faintly on old maps. It had no name now. Only bones of timber, blackened chimneys, and fields salted with ash.

They descended carefully, weapons drawn, though no enemy waited. What they found was worse.

Shapes lay twisted in the streets, villagers who had not fled fast enough. A child's toy lay half burned beside a small skeleton.

Lyra swore softly. Thalia knelt, trembling, her eyes shimmering with unshed tears. Brutus said nothing, jaw clenched as he limped past.

Kael stood in the village square, fist tightening. "We can't leave them like this," he said.

Thorne's voice came calm but hard. "We can't bury an entire village. Not without losing time."

"Then we bury who we can," Kael snapped. "If Malrik wants to turn the world to ash, then we fight him by remembering the lives he erased."

Lyra sighed but nodded. "Then let's get to work."

They dug with whatever they could find, broken shovels, planks, even bare hands. Kael carried the small skeleton himself, laying it in the earth with trembling care.

When the last grave was filled, dusk painted the sky crimson. They stood in silence, the wind sighing through ruins.

Then Brutus staggered, nearly falling. Thalia caught him, panic flashing in her eyes. The black veins had spread further.

"We need to move," she said. "Now. We need to get him to a healer, or he won't last another day."

Lyra called them over to a scorched wall. Burned deep into the stone was a sigil, a twisted mark of blackened runes.

Thalia's face paled. "The Flame of the Witherlands sigil. This village wasn't raided. It was claimed."

Kael stared at it, fury tightening his throat. "Then let this be our message in return." He spat into the ashes. "We're coming."

They left under nightfall, their lanterns dimmed, the mountains rising behind them like jagged tombstones.

At the ridge, Kael turned back one last time. The graves lay beneath the moonlight, silent and small.

"You'll be remembered," he whispered. "All of you."

The wind carried the words, scattering them across the ash. Then, from far off in the hills, came a sound.

A howl. Low, drawn, and hungry.

Then another. And another. Dire wolves. Malrik's hunters.

Kael's hand went to his sword as Thorne's voice rumbled behind him. "Seems the next trials found us, boy."

Kael exhaled, his gaze hard as steel. "Then we face it head-on."

The night wind rose, and the howls grew nearer.

The war in the shadows was far from over.

Chapter 22 - The Hunt in the Hills

The howls cracked the night like splintering glass.

It rose from the east, low and long, and was answered by another closer by. Then a third, from the ridges above. The pack was circling.

Kael's hand tightened on his sword hilt. His heart thudded in his ears, but he forced his voice steady. "We move. Now."

Lyra was already stringing her bow, her eyes sharp and calculating. Thalia tightened her grip around Brutus's arm, helping him rise, though his weight dragged heavily against her. His face was pale in the lantern glow, sweat beading along his brow.

"Damn wolves picked the wrong night," Brutus muttered, though his voice was hoarse, his bravado crumbling beneath the shadow-wound that spread like black fire through his veins.

Thorne took up the rear, his blade unsheathed with a whisper. His eyes were narrowed, scanning the dark hills. "They're driving us," he murmured. "Cutting us from the valley road. If we hesitate, they'll hem us in."

Kael nodded once. "Then we won't hesitate."

They moved quickly, boots crunching on gravel and sparse grass, the hills rising like dark waves around them. The moon hung half-veiled in drifting clouds, casting the land in broken silver. Every shadow could have been a wolf. Every gust of wind carried the scent of ash and blood.

Lyra ran ahead, scouting the ridges, her bow drawn and ready. Thalia kept close to Brutus, whispering strengthening charms that lent him shreds of strength. Kael stayed at their side, his blade bare, while Thorne's presence anchored the rear like an iron wall.

The howls came again. Louder. Closer. This time Kael heard the thundering of paws against the earth, echoing along the hillsides.

"They're herding us," Lyra hissed as she rejoined them, her breath sharp. "They're pushing us toward the broken gorge."

"The gorge?" Kael frowned.

"Two valleys over. Sheer cliffs, no bridge left standing. If we're trapped there..."

Kael didn't need her to finish. The wolves were not only hunting. They were driving the prey into the pit.

"We'll outmaneuver them," he said. "Keep west. Stay high on the ridge. Don't let them box us in."

His voice was calm, but fear twisted cold inside him.

The pack struck before they reached the ridge.

A shadow blurred from the night, massive and fast, eyes burning pale in the moonlight. Lyra loosed an arrow mid-stride. It sank deep into the beast's chest, but momentum carried it forward. It slammed into her, snarling, claws raking.

Kael was already there, sword flashing. He struck in a brutal arc, severing its neck in a spray of dark blood. The wolf collapsed at Lyra's feet, twitching, its eyes fading to dull glass.

"Up!" Kael barked, hauling her upright.

She grinned fiercely despite the blood on her arm. "One down."

But already two more shadows crested the ridge above, their howls shaking the stones.

Thorne met them, his blade sweeping in a wide arc. Steel sang as he carved one open along the flank, dodging the snapping jaws of the second. His movements were efficient and practiced, his expression grim.

The hills came alive with snarls.

“Go!” Thorne shouted. “I’ll hold them!”

Kael’s gut twisted. “Not alone.”

“Move, boy!” Thorne growled, his sword clashing against teeth and claw. “If they pin us here, none of you will leave this hill alive!”

Reluctantly, Kael obeyed, dragging the others forward, though every step felt like betrayal.

By the time they crested the western ridge, Brutus stumbled. His body faltered as though the earth itself dragged him down. He coughed, a wet sound, and collapsed to one knee.

“Brutus!” Thalia’s hands glowed violet as she pressed against his chest. The light sank into him, slowing the spread of black veins for a moment, but her face was pale, lips trembling.

“It’s burning me,” Brutus rasped. His eyes were bloodshot, glazed with fever. “Feels like fire crawling in my veins.”

Kael knelt, gripping his shoulder. “Hold on. Just hold on.”

Brutus gave a rough laugh that turned to a cough. “Don’t make that face, pup. I’ve walked with death on my heels before.” His hand tightened on Kael’s wrist with surprising strength. “But you... don’t fall. You're the reason we're still breathing.”

Before Kael could answer, another howl tore the night. Closer than ever.

Lyra's head snapped up. "They're flanking. We've got minutes, maybe less."

Kael rose, teeth gritted. They couldn't carry Brutus and outpace the pack. But they couldn't leave him either.

Every choice cut deep.

They reached a jagged break in the ridge where the earth had split ages ago, leaving a narrow ravine that wound like a scar. Kael led them down into it, the walls rising on either side. It was risky, but it forced the wolves to come from the front.

They made their stand in the ravine.

Kael planted himself at the entrance, sword raised, Lyra at his side with her bow. Thalia crouched with Brutus deeper inside, her hands glowing as she fought to slow the venom's march through his veins.

The first dire wolf lunged into the ravine, its jaws snapping like a bear trap. Lyra's arrows flew, finding the soft gaps beneath ribs and eyes. Still, more wolves pressed in, their hunger outweighing fear.

Then a deeper roar split through the night. Not a wolf's.

From the ridge above, a massive wolf corpse tumbled down, crashing into the ravine floor with a sickening thud. Standing in its wake was a broad, familiar silhouette.

"Thorne!" Kael shouted, relief sparking in his chest.

The old general descended the slope like a storm given flesh, his sword dripping with black blood. Another wolf leapt at him from the side, but Thorne met it mid-air, driving his blade clean through its chest. He landed in the ravine with the grace of a man half his age, eyes burning with the old fire.

“Miss me?” Thorne growled, yanking his sword free.

Kael allowed himself the smallest grin. “Took your time.”

“Had to clear the straggler,” Thorne said, sliding into formation beside him. “Can’t have them nipping at our heels while we finish this.”

The wolves hesitated now, circling, sensing the shift. With Thorne at their side, the line was unbroken.

Another wolf came, then another. Lyra’s arrows struck true, dropping one with a shaft through the eye. Thorne’s blade split another from throat to belly. Kael fought like a storm, his strikes fueled not only by training but by desperation. Every wolf that slipped past him meant death for the others.

The ravine floor ran slick with blood. Still, the pack did not falter.

The howls ceased. For a moment the night was still, broken only by the ragged breaths of men and beasts alike. Then, from the ridge above, it appeared.

The alpha.

It stood taller than a horse, its fur silver-shot and bristling, scars crisscrossing its massive frame. Its eyes glowed like coals, intelligent and merciless. When it growled, the earth itself seemed to rumble.

Kael felt his throat tighten. This was no mere beast. Malrik had touched it. Shaped it.

The alpha leapt down into the ravine. The ground shook where it landed.

“Kael!” Thorne barked, shifting his stance.

But the alpha ignored the old general. Its gaze fixed on Kael. As though it knew him. As though it marked him.

The wolf lunged.

Kael barely raised his sword in time. The force of the impact hurled him backward against the stone wall. Pain ripped through his ribs, his sword arm screaming as he locked his blade against the beast’s snapping jaws. Its breath stank of rot. Its eyes burned into him.

Lyra slinged an arrow. It struck the alpha’s flank, but the beast barely flinched. Thorne’s blade slashed its shoulder, opening flesh, but it spun with terrifying speed, knocking him aside with a swipe of its claw.

The alpha bore down on Kael.

Then Brutus roared.

The sound shook the ravine, raw and furious. He staggered to his feet, axe gripped in both hands, his body trembling from fever and venom but his eyes blazing with defiance.

“Come here, you cursed mutt!” he bellowed.

The alpha turned, lips curling back.

Brutus charged.

The axe came in a thunderous swing, biting deep into the wolf’s hind leg. The beast snarled, spinning to crush him, but Brutus held fast, his teeth gritted, veins black with shadow.

"Run!" he shouted, spitting blood. "Don't waste my final stand. Run!"

Kael's heart wrenched. Every instinct screamed to go to him, to fight beside him. But Thalia was already dragging at his arm, eyes wide with terror.

"Kael, we can't save him!"

The alpha reared, its massive form looming over Brutus.

For a heartbeat, Brutus met Kael's eyes across the blood-slick stones. A grin split his battered face.

"Tell Malrik... I'll be waiting for him in the pit."

The wolf descended.

Kael's roar echoed in the ravine as Thorne wrenched him back, forcing him to retreat. Lyra loosed arrow after arrow, covering their escape as the wolves surged in to join the slaughter.

They fled through the ravine, the sounds of Brutus's last stand thundering behind them. Roars, snarls, the clash of axe against claw, until the noise ended in a silence that carved Kael's soul raw.

They did not stop until the ravine widened into a slope of broken rock. The surviving wolves had not pursued. Perhaps Brutus's sacrifice had bought them more than time.

They collapsed there, breath ragged, hearts broken.

Kael sank to his knees, his sword slipping from numb fingers. His chest heaved, but his lungs felt empty. Brutus's voice still rang in his ears. His grin. His roar. His last words.

Lyra stood with her back against the stones, her face pale, eyes shining with fury and grief. Thalia sobbed openly, her hands shaking as the violet light guttered out.

Thorne said nothing, his face carved from stone, but his hand rested heavy on Kael's shoulder.

The night was silent again. Too silent.

Kael clenched his fists until his nails cut his palms. "We'll make it count," he whispered. His voice broke, but he did not care. "Brutus will not be forgotten. Malrik will pay for every life he's taken."

The vow burned in him like fire, fiercer than grief, fiercer than fear.

Above them, the moon broke free of the clouds, its light spilling across the hills. A cold witness to the price already paid.

Chapter 23 - Ashes of Brotherhood

The hills were too quiet.

The night after the wolf hunt, the air itself felt heavy, as though it shared in their grief. No crickets sang. No wind stirred the tall grass. Only the smoldering hush of what they had lost hung around them, a weight pressing so hard it threatened to crush their lungs.

Kael walked at the front of the group, but his feet felt like stone. Each step seemed to drag chains behind him. His hand rested on the hilt of his sword, but he no longer knew if it gave him strength or only reminded him of his failure. Behind him, Lyra and Thalia trudged wordlessly, their silence louder than any scream.

Brutus's absence was everywhere. In the rhythm of their march. In the uneven sound of their breaths. In the yawning hole where laughter should have been. The memory of him, his axe raised against the wolves, his roar defiant even as fangs closed in, burned in Kael's mind like a wound that refused to heal.

He had promised himself he would never lose another companion to Malrik's shadow. And yet, he had. His hand trembled on the hilt of his blade.

"Kael," Lyra said softly from behind, but he did not answer. He could not. Not yet.

When they finally stopped at a ridge to rest, no one spoke for a long time. They sat in the grass, each one staring at the ground as though afraid to look at the others.

Lyra hugged her knees, her bow resting at her side. Her face was pale in the dim light, streaked with dirt and sweat, her eyes rimmed red. Thalia sat with her hands pressed together, her lips moving soundlessly. A prayer or a desperate attempt to keep from shaking apart.

Kael paced. He wanted to say something, anything, but the words caught in his throat. A leader should have words. A leader should hold them together. That was what he had told himself when the journey began.

But now he had nothing.

Finally, Lyra broke the silence. "He should still be here." Her voice cracked on the last word.

Kael stopped pacing. His jaw clenched. "I know."

"Then why isn't he?" Her words began desperate but turned sharp as her grief spilled out. "You were leading us, Kael. You told us we'd make it. That if we followed you, we'd survive. But Brutus..."

"Enough," Kael snapped, the word harsher than he intended. Lyra flinched but did not back down.

"Don't tell me to be silent. Don't pretend this is just another scar we carry forward." Her eyes burned into his, wet with fury and grief. "We trusted you."

Kael's chest heaved. The guilt inside him roared for release, but all he could do was stare back, unable to give her what she needed.

A choked sob broke the tension. Thalia had sunk to her knees by the fire, her trembling hands covering her face. Tears streamed freely down her cheeks as she shook her head, words tumbling out between gasps.

"If I'd been stronger... if I hadn't drained myself fighting in those tunnels, I could have stopped it. I could have purged the shadow venom before it spread."

She looked up then, eyes bloodshot, voice trembling. "Brutus would still be here. Maybe all of them would. Damn it! If I'd just been better."

Kael turned toward her, his expression softening even as his own pain burned behind his eyes. "Thalia..."

She shook her head, curling in on herself, her voice breaking completely. "I was supposed to protect you all. That's what my gift is for. And I failed. Maybe my gift is a curse after all."

The fire cracked between them, the sound cruelly ordinary against her sobs.

It was Thorne's voice that finally cut through the storm.

"Let him breathe, girl," he said to Lyra. Then he looked at Thalia, his tone gentler. "And you, stop blaming what no mortal could change. The shadow venom was meant to kill. No healer could have undone it alone."

Thalia's sobs quieted, but the tears did not stop. Lyra bit her lip but said nothing more, turning away to hide her tears. Kael stood frozen, his hand trembling near his sword hilt, every word and every death pressing down like iron.

Kael lowered his head. "She's right," he muttered. "I told Brutus I'd keep him safe. I told all of you that." His voice broke. "But I couldn't. I wasn't strong enough."

Thorne pushed himself to his feet, joints popping in protest. He walked to Kael, slow but steady, and rested a scarred hand on the younger man's shoulder.

"Strength alone does not keep men alive, boy."

Kael swallowed hard. "Then what does?"

Thorne studied him for a long moment before answering. "Purpose. And the will to carry it, even when it breaks you."

Kael looked up, searching his mentor's face. "But Brutus is gone. How am I supposed to carry this? How am I supposed to lead them when I couldn't save him?"

Thorne's grip tightened. "Leadership is not about saving everyone. It is about walking the path even when you know you will lose people along the way." His voice dropped, rough with memory. "I've buried more men than I care to count. Brothers, friends, family. If I had let their deaths chain me down, I would never have stood again. And the enemy would have swallowed everything I loved."

Kael's chest heaved. "So I'm supposed to accept it? Just move on?"

"No." Thorne shook his head, his eyes fierce. "You remember him. You honor him. But you do not let his death rot you from the inside. You turn it into fire. You make sure every step forward carries his name with it. That is what it means to lead."

Later, as they made camp in the lee of the ridge, Kael sat apart, staring at the faint glow of the embers. His sword lay across his knees, gleaming faintly in the light.

Lyra sat across the flames, quiet now, her anger faded into raw grief. Thalia slept fitfully, whispering in her dreams.

Thorne sat beside Kael, pulling his cloak tighter against the night chill.

"You carry their trust," the old general said. "And their doubts. Both are heavier than a blade."

Kael nodded slowly. "I don't know if I can bear it."

"You can. Or you wouldn't be here still." Thorne's gaze turned to the stars. "Do you know what I learned long ago? A leader without values is nothing more than a tyrant. Malrik is proof of that. Power alone will never bind people to you. It is your values, the flame inside you, that they will follow."

Kael turned to him. "And what if that flame goes out?"

Thorne looked at him, and for the first time Kael saw not just the hardened general but the weary man beneath. "Then you borrow the flame of those beside you until yours burns again. That is why we do not walk alone."

Kael's throat tightened. The crushing guilt eased slightly, not gone, but tempered by something steadier. He thought of Brutus's booming laugh, his unshakable shield, his loyalty. If he gave in to despair, Brutus's sacrifice would mean nothing. He whispered to himself, quiet but firm, "I'll make this count."

The next morning, before they set out, Kael gathered them at a rise overlooking the valley. There, with rough stones and scraped earth, they built a cairn. Brutus's shattered shield, which Thalia had recovered, leaned against it.

Lyra's hands shook as she tied a strip of cloth to the stones. Thalia whispered a prayer, her violet eyes shining with tears.

When it was done, Kael stood before the cairn. His voice was steady, though his heart trembled.

"Brutus gave his life for us. For me. I will not let that be forgotten. We carry him with us, every step, every breath. He is part of this fight now. And I swear, by my crown and by my blood, I will make his sacrifice matter."

Silence followed, but it was no longer hollow. It was something heavier, something shared.

Lyra reached out and touched Kael's arm. Thalia stepped closer, her expression softer. Even Thorne gave a small nod, the faintest ghost of approval in his weathered face.

Together, they stood before the cairn. When they finally turned away, Kael felt the weight of his sword differently. Not as a burden, but as a promise.

They pressed on through the hills, shadows dogging their every step. At times Kael thought he heard wolves howling in the distance. Whether real or born of Malrik's malice, he could not tell. But he no longer walked with his head bowed.

Each step was agony, but each step was Brutus's legacy carried forward.

And though doubt still gnawed at him, Kael held fast to Thorne's words. It is not your blade they'll follow, but your flame.

For the first time, Kael began to believe that flame was real. And he vowed it would never go out.

Interlude - Echoes of a Shield

The cairn lay behind them now, a mound of stones marking Brutus's final stand. But Kael's heart had not moved forward.

That night, while the others slept in uneasy silence, he sat alone by the dwindling fire. The flames snapped and hissed, sparks vanishing into the dark sky, and in their light Kael found his mind pulled backward to a memory so vivid it hurt to hold.

It had been weeks before the wolf hunt, when the road was still hard but not yet carved with so many scars. They had camped near a brook, the summer air soft with crickets and fireflies.

Brutus had been the loudest thing in the night, as always. He had insisted on cooking despite Lyra's protests that he would burn the stew again, and had produced something thick, smoky, and nearly inedible.

"By the gods, Brutus, did you cook this in the ashes?" Lyra gagged after her first bite, making a face that nearly had Thalia spitting hers back into the bowl.

Brutus only roared with laughter, his shoulders shaking, eyes gleaming in the firelight. "That, lass, is the taste of strength. Puts hair on your chest. Even Kael will grow some whiskers after this."

Kael had tried to scowl, tried to remain the stoic leader, but the corner of his mouth betrayed him. Before he could stop it, he was laughing too, laughter that spilled from his chest like it had been waiting years to escape.

Thorne had only muttered into his beard, "If strength came from bad stew, you'd be king already," though even the old general allowed the faintest curve of a smile.

It had been a rare night, one where the shadow of Malrik felt distant and the group felt less like survivors and more like a family.

Kael remembered how Brutus had slapped his back so hard his ribs nearly cracked. “See, pup? Even kings need to laugh. Otherwise, what's the point of fighting?”

Kael pressed a hand against his eyes, willing the memory to fade before it tore him open. But the firelight kept painting Brutus’s grin across the darkness, kept echoing the sound of his booming voice.

The hills around him felt hollow without it.

He whispered aloud, voice ragged, “You were supposed to be at my side when I took the throne. You promised, Brutus.”

The night gave no answer. Only the crack of the fire and the weight of absence.

Soft steps approached. Kael glanced up to see Lyra, her bow slung across her shoulder, her hair loose around her face. She sat beside him without a word, watching the flames.

After a long silence, she spoke. “Do you remember that night by the brook? When he ruined the stew?”

Kael’s throat tightened. “I was just thinking of it.”

Lyra’s lips trembled, but a small smile touched them. “I’ve never seen you laugh like that.”

Kael looked down, shame and grief wrestling inside him. “I don’t know if I’ll ever laugh like that again.”

Lyra’s gaze was steady. “Then Brutus would be mad.”

Kael turned sharply to her, but she only shrugged. "He always said joy was the one weapon Malrik couldn't take away from us. Remember? He would mock you until you cracked a smile, just to prove it." Her voice caught, softer now. "He wouldn't want us to break apart because of him."

Kael swallowed hard. He wanted to believe her. He wanted to hold on to that memory, to let it strengthen rather than wound.

But the hole in his chest still yawned wide.

When Lyra drifted back to her bedroll, Kael remained awake, staring at the stars.

His thoughts circled, stubborn and refusing to rest. Brutus's death had been brutal, wolves tearing at his body, but Kael had not seen his body fall. The chaos of the battle had swallowed him whole.

What if...

The thought whispered like a dangerous spark in his mind. What if he survived?

It was impossible. And yet Kael could almost see it. Brutus crawling from the wolves, bloodied but alive, refusing to yield. He had always been too stubborn to die easily. Perhaps even now he was wandering, searching for them, cursing Kael's name for leaving him behind.

The ember of hope was small and fragile, but Kael clung to it.

He whispered to the night, voice hoarse, "If you're out there, Brutus, find me. Please."

The stars gave no answer, but Kael thought he felt something stir within him, the faintest echo of Brutus's shield, the faintest memory of his laughter.

And for the first time since the cairn, Kael let himself believe, if only for a heartbeat, that this was not the end of Brutus's story.

Chapter 24 - The Ashen Path

The hills bled into gray.

What little grass still clung to life came up brittle under their boots, snapping like old bones, the color drained to a lifeless pallor. Even the wind seemed dry, scraping across the rocks as though scouring the world of sound itself. The sky was not yet the Witherlands black horizon, but already it bore the warning, heavy ash-colored clouds straining against the sun, bleeding red light into the mist.

Kael marched in silence, his shoulders tight beneath his cloak. His sword hung at his side, though his hand strayed to it more often than he realized. It was not fear alone but a constant readiness, the instinct of someone who knew enemies could emerge from the shadow of any stone.

Behind him, the others followed with weariness written in every line of their bodies. Lyra's bow was slung across her back, her eyes scanning the broken ridges. Thalia walked with deliberate grace, but her face betrayed exhaustion, her violet eyes dulled with strain. And Thorne, steady and towering, kept his place at the rear, his gaze less on the land ahead and more on the group itself, guarding them from faltering.

It had been days since Brutus had vanished into the maw of the wolf pack. Days since Kael had felt the sickening helplessness of watching a comrade swallowed by the wild. No body had been recovered. No howl in the night had carried his return.

And yet Kael's heart resisted closing the door. Brutus was too stubborn to die. Or so Kael told himself, though it felt more like pressing on a wound to feel pain than seeking comfort.

They had buried their grief in movement. The path toward the Witherlands allowed no pause, no mourning. And so, the Ashen Path became their grave marker, each mile walked a silent prayer.

By noon, the hills funneled into a narrow cut of stone, the wind howling through like the voice of something trapped beneath the earth. Kael raised a hand, slowing their pace.

“Something’s wrong,” he murmured.

Lyra was already nocking an arrow. “I’ve felt it since dawn. We’re being followed.”

Thalia’s fingers flexed at her side, faint sparks crackling where her magic itched to be called. “By what?”

Thorne answered grimly. “Not wolves. Not men either. Listen.”

They did. For a moment only silence filled the ravine. Then Kael heard it, the low scrape of claws over stone, too deliberate to be the wind. A rasping breath, just out of sight.

The group closed ranks instinctively. From the shadows ahead, the first of the creatures emerged.

It was shaped like a hound but twisted, its body stretched thin as parchment, skin grey and tattered like smoke clinging to bone. Its eyes glowed a sickly ember-orange, and its jaws dripped not saliva but black ichor that hissed against the stone. Behind it came three more, their bodies flickering faintly as though not fully part of this world.

“Wraith-hounds,” Thorne growled, drawing steel. “Scouts of the Witherlands.”

They came without warning, rushing forward with shrieks that curdled the air.

Kael's sword met the first with a ringing clash, sparks spitting as though he had struck iron instead of flesh. The impact jolted his arm to the shoulder, but he braced, twisting to drive his blade through the creature's throat. Instead of blood, smoke poured out, searing his lungs as he gasped.

Lyra's arrow sang, piercing the skull of a hound mid-leap. It dissolved into ash before it even struck the ground. Thalia thrust her hand forward, violet fire bursting from her palm. The flames caught on another hound's side, but rather than burning, the creature howled as its form unraveled, as though the fire stripped away the shadow that bound it.

Still, more poured from the cracks in the ravine. A dozen. Two dozen.

"Back to the rocks!" Kael shouted. "Don't let them surround us."

They fought shoulder to shoulder, the narrow pass their only salvation. Thorne cleaved through the hounds with brutal precision, each strike scattering smoke and embers. Lyra loosed arrow after arrow, never missing, though her quiver ran perilously low. Thalia's fire painted the air violet, searing back the tide.

And Kael moved at the center, blades striking in rhythm not with desperation but with command. His voice rang out over the chaos, steady, directing, leading.

"Thalia, left flank. Lyra, take the high ones. Thorne, with me."

For the first time since Brutus's fall, the group moved as one. Not broken pieces, but a whole.

The last hound fell shrieking, its form unraveling into a pool of tar that hissed into the cracks. The air hung thick with smoke and rot. Kael lowered his sword slowly, chest heaving.

None of them spoke for a long moment. The silence after battle was louder than the clash itself.

Lyra was the first to break it. “Scouts only,” she said softly. “If those were ahead of us, the rest know we're coming.”

Thalia’s lips pressed thin. “The Witherlands already reach for us.”

Kael’s gaze drifted to the horizon. He knew they were right. But he also knew retreat was no longer an option.

They found shelter that night in the hollow of a broken hill, where jagged cliffs shielded them from the wind. The campfire they built was small, its glow a fragile defiance against the surrounding dark.

Kael sat apart from the others at first, his sword laid across his knees. He could still feel the weight of command from earlier, the way his voice had steadied them. It both frightened and strengthened him.

Thorne joined him after a while, lowering himself to the ground with the sound of weary joints. “You’re thinking too loud,” the old warrior said.

Kael gave a faint smile, but it did not last. “I nearly led us to ruin. If the hounds had been more than scouts...”

“But they weren’t,” Thorne interrupted. “And you didn’t.” His eyes were steady, iron-grey in the firelight. “Leadership isn't about certainty, Kael. It’s about stepping forward when no one else will. Today, you did that.”

Kael’s hands tightened on the hilt of his sword. “And tomorrow? When the Witherlands stand before us? When Malrik’s generals strike?”

Thorne's silence was long, but it was not empty. At last he said, "Then you will step forward again. Even if your knees shake. Even if it costs you everything. That is the burden of kingship. And the gift."

Kael stared into the flames, the reflection dancing in his eyes. He wanted to argue, to say he wasn't ready, but the words died before they reached his tongue.

Across the fire, Lyra was tending her bowstring, though her gaze flicked often to Kael. Thalia sat with her back to the stone, eyes closed as though listening to something deeper than the night. They both carried their doubts, their griefs. And yet they remained. For him.

Kael swallowed hard. For the first time, he began to understand not just the cost of leadership, but the faith it demanded.

Near midnight, restless, Kael rose and wandered from the fire. The land sloped gently down toward the east, where the horizon burned faintly with a red glow. The Witherlands.

Half-buried in the soil nearby stood an old marker stone, cracked and weatherworn. The crest carved upon it was nearly erased, but Kael recognized it, the sun sigil of Elaria marking the border that once held Malrik's forces at bay. Now it was defiled, streaked with ash and black ichor.

Kael knelt before it. He touched the stone, feeling the rough edges against his palm.

"By the blood of my house," he whispered, "I vow we will see these lands restored. Not for the crown. Not for glory. But for those who have fallen, and those who still stand with me."

Behind him, footsteps crunched on the gravel. Lyra. She said nothing, but when Kael rose, he saw her gaze linger on him with a quiet fire. She had heard, and she believed.

Dawn broke faint and grey. They climbed the last ridge together, the wind biting, the air heavy with a scent like burned iron.

And there it was.

The Witherlands stretched before them, an endless expanse of charred earth and rivers of molten rock that glowed faintly beneath the crust. Blackened spires rose like claws from the ground, smoke curling from their tips. The sky itself seemed wounded, a bruise of red and shadow pressing down.

None of them spoke. Words would have cheapened the moment.

Kael's hand drifted to his sword. The blade felt heavier than ever, but also truer.

“This is where it begins,” he said softly.

Thorne rested his hand on his shoulder. “And where it must end.”

Together, they descended into the Witherlands.

Interlude – The Crown of Ash

The Hollow Mountains were graves carved into the sky. Their jagged summits loomed like black fangs, their valleys suffocated by endless fog that stank of sulfur and rot. Lightning often split their peaks, but no thunder followed; the sound seemed swallowed by the mountains themselves.

At their heart, Castle Noctis festered.

It was not a place built by mortal hands. No mason could have designed its crooked towers, no craftsman its serrated battlements. It looked as though the mountain itself had rotted from within and erupted outward in spires of obsidian. The air was thin, choked with ash that never settled, as if the land forever smoldered from some ancient fire.

Travelers who approached its gates, few as they were, spoke of hearing whispers before they saw the fortress. Screams that leaked from stone. Pleas for mercy long past. The walls seemed wet to the touch, not with rain but with condensation that reeked of iron and blood. Even the crows that circled were wrong, their eyes pale and blind, yet they never crashed against rocks.

Castle Noctis lived. It remembered. And it fed.

Inside, the corridors bled chill. Torches sputtered with greenish flame that offered no warmth. The floors shone with obsidian tiles polished to mirrors, reflecting faces wrong and distorted, as if the stone remembered every soul that had crossed it and twisted them in mockery.

Deep within, the throne hall waited.

Its ceiling arched like a ribcage, pillars shaped as if carved from giant bones. The throne itself was wrought of black iron fused with pale skulls, each one cracked and hollow-eyed, their mouths frozen in silent screams. Chains dangled from the rafters, some swaying though no draft stirred.

It was here that the true horror breathed.

The chains clattered as guards dragged the prisoner forward. His hands and feet were bound, his face a ruin of blood and dirt. He stumbled, tried to plead, but the words were beaten out of him before he reached the throne.

Malrik sat upon it like a king of carrion. His armor gleamed wetly, black steel veined with crimson, as though blood pulsed within the metal itself. His face was sharp and cold, pale as moonlight, his eyes a void that seemed to drink the flicker of torches.

The prisoner was thrown at his feet.

"Mercy, my lord," the man gasped, his voice ragged. "I brought warning of the heir, of Kael."

Malrik rose slowly. His shadow stretched across the hall like a living thing. He reached down, his iron gauntlet closing around the man's throat with the ease of a farmer plucking a reed.

"You speak of warnings," Malrik murmured, his voice deep as a tomb. "Do you think I fear shadows?"

The man kicked and gagged, his eyes bulging. Malrik lifted him higher until his spine cracked. In his other hand he summoned his blade, a great sword black as midnight, runes along its edges burning with a dull, hungry red.

The prisoner's screams grew faint as life drained. His eyes rolled, his body spasmed. Malrik did not strike. He only watched. Waiting. Listening to silence as the man died in his grasp.

When the body sagged, Malrik tossed it aside with casual contempt. The hall fell still again. Only then did the great doors creak open.

Virex entered alone.

Her armor was deep crimson-black. Heat shimmered faintly around her, distorting the air; even her silent steps left a sense of smoldering weight behind. She spoke nothing. She simply knelt, her helm shaped like a serpent's maw, her presence as heavy as the stone walls themselves.

Malrik's gaze lingered on her, and the faintest curl of satisfaction touched his lips.

"You burn with patience," he rumbled, stepping down from his throne, his shadow stretching long across the hall. "The others would waste themselves on fire and fury. But you, Virex, you endure. You wait. That is why I send you."

She did not raise her head.

"Return to the Witherlands," Malrik commanded, his voice a dark echo in the chamber. "The boy will come. He and his little band of strays think themselves brave enough to tread your ash-choked roads. When they do, you will meet them."

His eyes narrowed, the steel of his will pressing down like a blade. "Do not kill him. Break him. Bind him. Bring him to me."

For a moment, the molten seams of her armor pulsed brighter, as though her very blood flared in answer. Then, silent as ever, Virex bowed lower, accepting the command.

Malrik turned away, his cloak whispering like a shadowed flame.

"Go, Flame of the Witherlands," he said. "And let the boy learn what it means to choke on ash."

Later, Malrik climbed the highest spire of Castle Noctis. Alone.

Here, the wind cut like knives, yet even the storm gave him distance. From this height, he could see the world beyond the Hollow Mountains. In the far distance, faint lights glimmered where Elaria still lived.

He hated them.

He remembered the palace's marble halls, its sunlit windows. The laughter of courtiers, the songs of festivals. He remembered standing in that city once, as a boy, not as Malrik, not as warlord, but as a nameless wretch ignored by their shining royalty.

They had called his people beasts. Vermin. Tainted by blood not fit for thrones.

They had been wrong.

Now he wore their king's crown as a bauble on his throne room floor, broken and scorched. Yet it was not enough.

No. The crown he sought was more. Older. The Dragonfire Crown. A relic that had crowned Elaria's dragon-kings for centuries, said to hold the fire of the first dragon. It had vanished in the flames when the palace fell. Malrik had searched, torn apart stone and bone alike, yet still it eluded him.

But he could feel it.

It called to him in dreams. It whispered in the blood he spilled. He would have it. And when it burned upon his brow, there would be no dawn. Only night.

When Malrik slept, dreams came.

He was back in Elaria. The palace burned. Its white towers cracked, windows bleeding fire. The screams of men, women, and children filled the air, but to him it was music.

He remembered walking the hall of kings, his blade dripping. He remembered the queen's cry as he cut her down, the king's fury silenced beneath steel. He remembered the little prince, dragged from the cradle of his mother's corpse.

But the dream shifted. The child did not die.

Instead, he stood before Malrik, grown, a sword in hand. Kael. His eyes burned not with fear but with fury. The palace flames did not consume him; they crowned him, wreathed him in fire that did not burn.

And upon his head, the Dragonfire Crown.

Malrik awoke with a growl, his hand clenched on his blade. The spire shuddered as if the mountain itself recoiled from his rage.

He descended into the deepest chamber of Castle Noctis. Few knew it existed.

There, in a vault carved of black stone, stood a pedestal. Upon it rested nothing. Yet the air shimmered, burned, as though something unseen waited.

Malrik knelt before it.

"My crown," he whispered, voice hoarse and reverent. "You will be mine. With you, I will unmake kingdoms. With you, I will burn the last hope from this world. With you, I will be eternal."

The shadows stirred. The stone walls hissed like voices. And in the silence, it seemed the unseen crown whispered back.

Chapter 25 - Flame of the Witherlands

The heat struck first.

It rolled off the land in waves, oppressive and searing, until even breath felt like smoke drawn into the lungs. Each step into the Witherlands was a battle against the air itself, thick with ash that coated the tongue and burned the eyes. Beneath their boots, the ground cracked and crumbled, riddled with veins of molten fire glowing faintly through the stone.

Kael's cloak stuck to his back with sweat, the sword at his side hot enough to blister skin. Still, he pressed forward, his gaze locked on the horizon, where black spires clawed at a bruised red sky.

No one spoke. The land silenced them. Lyra moved with her bow at the ready, though even she faltered against the heat. Thalia's skin glistened, but her eyes remained sharp, her magic stirring faint sparks as though the oppressive air itself tried to draw it out. And Thorne, steady and indomitable, grimaced with every step, though he bore it without complaint.

The silence broke only when Lyra whispered, "We're being watched."

Kael already knew. He had felt it since they crossed the ridge, an awareness lingering beyond sight, the way a forest feels the predator's eyes.

Then the land answered.

From the cracks in the ground, fire flared. Figures emerged, armored in blackened steel that seemed forged from the land itself. Their helmets bore twisted visors, and their weapons burned with an inner heat, glowing faintly like brands. Dozens, no hundreds, ringed the ridge ahead, their formation perfect, their discipline unshaken even in the haze. Kael's group halted.

A path opened among the soldiers, and through it came a sound: not footsteps, but the grinding scrape of steel over stone. A figure walked between the ranks, her presence more oppressive than the heat itself.

She stood taller than Kael, her armor a deep crimson black, every plate traced with molten lines as though lava itself flowed through her veins. Her helm bore a crown of jagged horns, and when she removed it, a mane of ember-red hair spilled out, wild and burning. Her skin bore the mark of fire, bronzed and scarred in places yet made beautiful by the sheer authority she carried.

Her eyes were the worst, two flames burning in sockets that had once been human, now molten gold, fierce and consuming.

General Virex. The Flame of the Witherlands.

"Elarian blood dares tread this land," she said, her voice low and resonant, each word echoing as though the Witherlands itself spoke through her. She smiled, and it was not kindness. "At last. The heir comes crawling to his pyre."

Kael's grip tightened on his sword. "General Virex."

"Child," she replied, almost gently. "You wear your father's steel. You carry your people's hopes. And yet you march into my dominion, blind to the price."

Her smile deepened. She gestured behind her.

The soldiers shifted, dragging something forward from the haze. Kael's heart turned to ice.

There, on their knees, bound in chains, beaten and bloodied, were Sera, Ryo, Kester, Eran, and Marra. The last of Emberdeep's fighters who had followed them into the wastes. Their faces were swollen and bruised, their clothes charred and torn.

One of them, Eran, was missing his right arm, the wound wrapped in scorched bandages. Kester barely stirred, his head hanging low, blood dripping onto the cracked earth.

Lyra gasped softly, a sound more pain than breath. Thalia covered her mouth, her eyes wide with horror.

Virex's voice slithered through the silence. "Your rebellion dies as it lived, on its knees."

Thorne's jaw tightened, his hand flexing over his sword. "You've no honor, witch."

Her gaze slid to him like a blade. "Honor is for those who win. You should have learned that when you fled your king's pyre, old wolf."

Kael's blade rasped from its sheath. "Enough."

The word rang sharper than steel. His companions drew as one, Lyra's bowstring taut, Thalia's palms blazing with violet fire, Thorne's greatsword gleaming even against the oppressive light.

Virex spread her arms, unarmed, the fire at her back rising in answer. "So be it. Come, little prince. Let me burn away your illusions."

The soldiers closed, their formation moving like a tide of steel. Kael surged forward, his blade clashing with the first of Virex's guard. The strike sent sparks flying, the sound deafening in the dry air.

Lyra's arrows flew in rapid succession, each finding its mark, although the soldiers fought on, their armor seeming to drink the shafts of wood and steel. Thalia's flames burst outward in waves, violet fire colliding with the crimson blaze of the Witherlands. The ground trembled under the clash of magics.

Thorne roared, cleaving through three at once, his great sword glowing red from the heat of their armor.

Then Virex moved.

She did not run or rush. She strode forward, and with each step, the air twisted, fire lashing out in whips that struck at Kael. He barely raised his sword in time, the force of the flame hitting harder than steel. The heat seared his arms, but he did not falter.

He lunged, blade aimed at her heart.

Her gauntlet caught it mid-strike, bare hand gripping the steel. The metal hissed, glowing orange beneath her touch. Her smile widened.

"Good," she whispered, and she hurled him back as if he weighed nothing.

Kael hit the ground hard, breath driven from his chest. Above him, Virex's shadow loomed, her hair blazing like a torch against the red sky.

As he rose again, she spoke, mocking and cruel.

"How did you like the village I burned on your way here?" she asked, her tone almost conversational. "The cries of the villagers were lovely. I almost kept one alive, just to thank me properly."

Kael's blood boiled hotter than the air around him. He charged with a roar, fury eclipsing pain.

Their blades clashed again, steel against fire. Every strike was agony, the heat searing through the hilt into his bones. But he pressed on, refusing to yield.

He struck high, low, feinted, spun, movements born of Thorne's training and desperation. Virex matched him effortlessly, her expression calm and almost amused.

"You fight well for a boy," she said, her voice smooth even in battle. She caught his blade again, twisted it aside, then drove her knee into his chest. Pain exploded through his ribs.

Still, Kael slashed upward, nicking her cheek. A single drop of blood welled and hissed into smoke against her skin.

Virex's smile vanished. Her eyes flared brighter. "You will learn your place."

Her palm struck his chest. Fire erupted point-blank, hurling him across the field. He skidded across the stone, his cloak aflame, his skin blistering where the fire kissed him.

"Kael!" Lyra's scream cut through the roar.

He forced himself up, teeth clenched, vision swimming. His sword still lay in his grip. Somehow, impossibly, he still stood.

Thalia staggered, collapsing as her magic guttered. Thorne fought with unrelenting fury, but even he was slowing, his great sword dragging. Lyra's quiver was empty, her bow useless against the unending tide.

Kael felt his body failing, the heat swallowing his strength, breaths turning shallow.

Virex walked toward him again, her soldiers parting like shadows before fire. Her voice carried over the battlefield, commanding and final.

"You are not your father. You are not a king. You are a child playing war. And now your crown burns."

She raised her hand. Fire gathered into a blazing spear.

Kael raised his sword. He would not bow. He would not yield.

The flames struck.

The impact drove him to his knees, his blade shattering under the force. Fire engulfed him, wrapping around his body like chains, searing and consuming, binding him in molten shackles.

"Kael!" Lyra cried, voice breaking. She tried to run to him, but soldiers seized her and dragged her back. Thorne bellowed in rage, only to be forced to the ground beneath a dozen blades. Thalia's scream turned into a sob as her magic failed entirely.

Virex stood over Kael, her burning eyes triumphant.

"The heir of Elaria," she proclaimed, her voice ringing like a death knell. "Captured. Broken. Delivered to the flame."

Kael struggled, but the fire held him fast, his vision dimming. The last thing he saw was the faces of his companions, struggling and helpless yet unyielding.

And behind them, the bodies of the fallen rebels, what remained of them, lit by the fires of the Witherlands.

Darkness closed in.

"To be continued…"

Thank you so much for reading Volume 1 of *Blade of the Fallen Crown*. I truly hope you enjoyed the journey as much as I did bringing it to life. This story is only the beginning, and I am excited to continue building this world and exploring the paths of these characters. Your support means everything, and I hope you will join me for the next chapter of this adventure. The crown may have fallen, but the fight to reclaim it has only just begun.

Jordan Beland

DEDICATION

To my mom.

I began writing this story while you were fighting through chemotherapy, putting words on a page was the way I knew how to quiet the fear and anxiety of watching someone I love go through so much. You passed away on November 18th after a brave, hard-fought battle, but your strength, love, and belief in me continue to guide every step I take. I will keep writing, keep growing, and keep creating, because I want to make you proud with every book I release. This one, and all the ones to come, are for you.

Blade of the Fallen Crown will return.

www.ingramcontent.com/pod-product-compliance
Lightning Source LLC
Chambersburg PA
CBHW070631310726
48982CB00001B/244

* 9 7 9 8 9 9 3 8 8 5 5 0 6 *